»»»»»»»»»»»»»»»»«««««««««««««««««

Evgeniya Tur
Antonina

TRANSLATED BY MICHAEL R. KATZ

INTRODUCTION BY JEHANNE GHEITH

NORTHWESTERN UNIVERSITY PRESS

EVANSTON, ILLINOIS

»»»»»»»»»»»»»»»»«««««««««««««««««

Northwestern University Press
Evanston, Illinois 60208-4210

Printed in the United States of America

isbn 0-8101-1407-0

Library of Congress Cataloging-in-Publication Data

Tur, Evgeniia, 1815–1892.
  [Antonina. English]
  Antonina / Evgeniya Tur ; translated by Michael R. Katz ;
introduction by Jehanne Gheith.
        p. cm. — (European classics)
  Vol. 3 of author's Plemiannitsa published in Moscow (1851)
and also under the title Antonina in the almanac "Kometa" (1851).
  Romanized record.
  isbn 0-8101-1407-0 (pbk. : alk. paper)
  I. Katz, Michael R. II. Title. III. Series: European classics
(Evanston, Ill.)
pg3418.t75a8513 1996
891.73'3—dc20   96-30760
                                                        cip

»»» CONTENTS «««

»»» ««««
Introduction
Jehanne Gheith

Evgeniya Tur, born Elizaveta Sukhovo-Kobylina (1815–92),[1] *was a prominent and influential author in the nineteenth century; she participated in nearly every institution of Russian letters (fiction, criticism, editing, children's literature, the salon) and was accomplished in all these areas.*[2] *Through her mother's Moscow salon, she was acquainted with many well-known intellectuals of her day. Her mother, Mariya Ivanovna (born Shepeleva), placed a high value on literature and the arts, and this emphasis told: Tur's brother, Aleksandr, was a well-known playwright and philosopher; their sister Sofiya was an artist and the first woman to win a gold medal from the Imperial Academy of Arts (1854). Many of the leading intellectuals and writers of Tur's day, including the historian Timofei Granovsky, the poet Nikolai Ogarev, and the author Ivan Turgenev, frequented her salon in the 1850s. Tur was considered a major new talent in 1849, when she published her first novella,* Oshibka (A Mistake), *but her reputation as an author of serious prose fiction soon faded.*[3] *She turned to other aspects of Russian letters: journalism, criticism, and children's fiction. Tur had an impressive career as a social and literary critic, writing insightful and widely respected articles on many topics and in many forums, including the most widely disseminated periodicals of the day, such as* Biblioteka dlya chteniya (Library for Reading), Otechestvennye zapiski (Notes of the Fatherland), Sovremennik (The Contemporary), *the Dostoevsky brothers'* Vremya (Time), *and the newspaper* Golos (The Voice). *From 1856 to 1860 she edited the belles-lettres section of Mikhail Katkov's* Russkii vestnik (The Russian Messenger). *In 1861 Tur founded, edited, and managed a periodical,* Russkaya rech (Russian Speech), *in which she attempted to define a middle ground between "aesthetic" and "radical" critics and between Slavophiles and Westernizers.[4] Tur is one of the few women known to have established a publication dealing in politics, history, and literature in this period.[5] In the mid-1860s Tur began writing fiction for children (mainly fairy tales or religious and/or historical novellas). Her children's fiction was highly regarded both by her contemporaries and by later generations, and her works for children and adults were read and remembered by Zinaida Gippius and Marina Tsvetaeva, among others.[6]*

"These pages . . . will remain in Russian literature," wrote Ivan Turgenev, referring to *Antonina* (1851);[7] other critics, too, praised the novella highly, rating it over works by Turgenev and other (now) better-known writers. But these pages did not remain in Russian literature, although, perhaps, they are now returning to it. That return offers rich possibilities for reimagining the Russian literary tradition.

Antonina first appeared in an almanac, *Kometa* (*The Comet*), together with works by Timofei Granovsky, Ivan Turgenev, Aleksandr Ostrovsky, and other prominent authors of the period. Writers published in this collection were then considered among Russia's best, and reviewers generally agreed that *Antonina* was the finest work in the volume.[8]

Most works of prose fiction by Russian women of the nineteenth century have shared the fate of *Antonina;* this prose is not part of the literary tradition as it is usually conceptualized and taught. It is difficult even to find works by Russian women – in Russian or in English. Few of these fictions have been reprinted since the 1917 revolution; thus they are available only in prerevolutionary orthography and in the so-called "thick journals," which are located only in university or other academic libraries (such as the Library of Congress or the major libraries in Russia).[9] Furthermore, very few prose fictions by nineteenth-century women writers have been translated. The publishing history of *Antonina* exemplifies these difficulties: Tur's novella has not been republished in Russia since 1851, and it is one of the few prose works by nineteenth-century Russian women writers to be translated into English.[10]

My main concern, however, is not why these works have been forgotten, but rather what historical understandings and new possibilities are opened up by restoring these fictions to Russian letters.[11] Reading *Antonina* and contemporary responses to it reveals a great deal not only about the culture and literature of the period, but also about the history and aesthetics of Russian women's writing. These are particularly important issues to explore given that the 1850s is a largely forgotten decade in Russian (literary) history and that, until recently, nineteenth-century women writers have been virtually left out of that history.

The case of *Antonina* suggests the extent to which women's writings[12] were an integral part of the nineteenth-century Russian literary tradition: the history of the novella demonstrates that women's fictions both influenced works by (now) better-known male authors and were influenced by them. Although I will discuss mainly Tur and Turgenev here, their relationship is not at all anomalous; many women writers had creative (and sometimes destructive) partnerships with male authors: Elena Gan and Osip Senkovsky, Anna Korvin-Krukovskaya and Fedor Dostoevsky, Avdotya Panaeva and

Nikolai Nekrasov, to name a few.[13] And although *Antonina* is but one example of Russian women's prose at midcentury, I see it as a case study; as readers explore the works of authors like Durova, Gan, Rostopchina, Pavlova, and the Khvoshchinskaya sisters, we can build an understanding of the place and significance of women's writings in Russian letters, which in turn demands rethinking traditional conceptualizations of Russian literature.[14]

Antonina is intimately bound up with two of Ivan Turgenev's works: *Dnevnik lishnego cheloveka* (*Diary of a Superfluous Man*, 1850) and *Neschastnaya* (*An Unfortunate Woman*, 1869).[15] Just before writing *Antonina* and just after reading *Diary of a Superfluous Man*, Tur wrote to Turgenev asking him to coauthor a novella with her.[16] Although the two never formally wrote anything together, they did read and discuss one another's drafts.[17] And, on one level, *Antonina* is a response to Turgenev. In her novella, Tur rewrites the superfluous man's *Diary*, focusing on the heroine's development and showing the male protagonist from the heroine's point of view; in so doing, Tur portrays the superfluous man in a new and unflattering light. In *An Unfortunate Woman*, as Jane Costlow has demonstrated, the influence went the other way, as Turgenev incorporated and reworked many aspects of Tur's *Antonina* in his novella.[18]

Turgenev was important not only in the conception of *Antonina*, but also in its reception. He reviewed Tur's *Plemyannitsa* (*The Niece*, 1851), the four-volume novel of which *Antonina* constitutes most of volume 3.[19] As is clear from the excerpt at the end of this volume, Turgenev held *Antonina* in high regard. But the way in which Turgenev structures his essay undercuts his praise and reinforces common stereotypes about women's writing.

Before turning to *Antonina*, Turgenev devotes much of his essay to describing writings by women – in largely negative terms. He notes, for example, that *The Niece* is verbose and claims that, in Russia, only a woman would undertake a four-volume novel; male authors would recognize that their country, at that historical moment, could not support or justify such prolixity.[20] Turgenev discusses female authorship not only in Russia, but also in general, and he sums up his lengthy discourse on the topic: "We simply affirm that in women's talents – and we don't exclude the greatest of these, George Sand – there is something not quite right, not literary, springing straight from the heart – not thought through to completion."[21] By calling women's writing "unliterary," Turgenev defines the literary as a male province. And as is clear from the rest of Turgenev's essay, the literary is to be prized by writers and readers. Having thus placed Tur's writing in the "automatically secondary" category, Turgenev then praises *Antonina,* but that praise will be read in the context of his earlier comments.[22] Praising and damning women's writing practically in the same breath was common in the late 1830s and has been repeated by most major critics of women's fiction in the mid-nineteenth century – and since.[23]

Turgenev's review of *Antonina* is typical of the way critics greeted writings by Russian women. The reception of *Antonina* rehearses some of the major assumptions made about fiction by women at the midcentury: women's prose was classed separately from that by men, and it was usually considered long-winded and "subjective," meaning that the author was too close to the fiction for true artistry. In addition, women's writings were thought to have limited social value. The influential critic Vissarion Belinsky claimed that women were unable to move beyond their "female and feminine" sphere and therefore were incapable of creating great art (both aesthetically and in terms of social significance). In such statements, Belinsky was expressing a common cultural and critical attitude; many other critics said or assumed similar precepts in discussing women's writings.[24]

Interpreting the gendered effects of criticism is complicated, for both men and women were affected by and responded to published critiques of their works. Yet examining Tur's response to Turgenev is richly suggestive for a more complete understanding of Russian women's writing. Although later commentators have largely regarded Turgenev's review as positive,[25] Tur herself strongly objected to it. Writing to a historian friend (Konstantin Bestuzhev-Ryumin),[26] she noted:

> I was very annoyed several days ago and even now I can't think without pain about Turgenev's criticism [of *The Niece*] in the first issue of *The Contemporary*. I don't like the tone. . . . parts of it are very strange – read it and judge for yourself; I think this criticism will do me harm. . . . It's not good, not at all good of Turgenev – it would have been better not to write anything than to write what he did. . . . I especially don't like the place where it says that only a woman could decide to write a novel in four parts and many other places where he talks about chattering, etc. Read it carefully, you'll see that the article is clever but nasty and tricky to the highest degree and deeply offensive. It is Iv[an] Serg[eevich] [Turgenev] to the hilt with his apparent kindness, but, in fact, his poisonous kindness. It upset me a lot. I am completely unable to work.[27]

Tur, then, found Turgenev's criticism much more compelling than his praise,[28] and his article made it difficult for her to write. It could be argued that participation in the field of Russian letters demanded a certain level of imperviousness to criticism, since exchanges of the period were often fiercely brilliant (for example, the polemics between Shchedrin and Dostoevsky). But it is more illuminating to examine Tur's statement as a guide to deeper understandings of a woman writer's position in nineteenth-century Russia. Her letter provides information about several issues including what facilitated women's participation in the literary tradition, what worked against it, and how criticism affected women's writing. The fact that Turgenev's review was published in one of the most widely read journals of the day, while Tur's response took the form of a private letter, is itself indicative: what has resonated through Russian letters is (largely) the male critique, not the female response.[29]

Although I have said that negative criticism made it difficult for Tur to write, I do not want to imply that negative criticism was difficult only for women: Dostoevsky and Leskov are two obvious counterexamples. Nor do I want to suggest that women were fainting flowers, unable to meet the tough demands of the nineteenth-century literary arena. The issues, I think, were different for men and women, as were their positions vis-à-vis writing: as Turgenev's essay suggests, women had to prove they belonged to the realm of the "literary" – and they had to do so against the powerful weight of societal opinion, much of which they had internalized (countless letters by Russian women question whether they can legitimately be considered authors).[30] This means that, for many women, including Tur, coming to authorship meant constantly engaging the societal norm that stated that "women" and "writers" were mutually exclusive categories. Women responded variously to these social mores, but the fact of having to deal with them was a constant feature of the literary landscape for nineteenth-century Russian women authors, and it affected both their fictional writings and their response to criticism.

As noted above, it was generally agreed that women's fictions did not contribute to social progress – and this at a time (1840s–60s) when it was commonly believed that the primary role of literature was as an agent of social transformation. Actually reading prose fiction by Russian women, however, reveals that their works forcefully criticize societal norms, although, as we shall see, often in different ways from the fictions of authors like Pushkin, Gogol, and Dostoevsky. *Antonina*, for example, provides both a powerful social critique and elaborates an important aesthetic.[31]

Antonina is an extended society tale, a genre most commonly associated with Russia of the 1830s. The plot will be familiar to readers of *Jane Eyre* (1847), of whom Tur was one.[32] The eponymous heroine is an orphan raised by two stepparents; her stepmother is a governess, and Antonina herself later becomes a governess and marries a wealthy man. Most of Tur's novella describes Antonina's relationship with her beloved, Michel. Breaking with the *Jane Eyre* plot, Michel is a man of great tenderness and limited decisiveness, and the young couple is separated by the combination of his weak will and the forces of propriety, which do not approve of matches between *sosloviya* (estates).[33] Eventually, Antonina marries another and becomes a stepmother, mother, and music teacher.

There are some spectacularly unlikely elements in *Antonina*. The heroine is raised not by one, but by two evil stepparents; in addition, the dynamics of nationality in her family relationships are intensely complicated. Antonina's biological father is German, her stepmother, French, and her stepfather, English. Antonina first falls in love with a Russian whose name, Michel, she always pronounces in French (as was the custom of the day); she later marries an Italian businessman, Albert Bertini. These characters are stereotypic, as was pointed out at the time.[34] For example, the English stepfather is a cold, calculating disciplinarian, the Italian husband, extremely passionate and sexually aggressive. But even if stereotypic, this interplay of nationalities shows Russians in relationship to, influenced by, and influencing other nationalities. *Antonina* depicts a young Russian woman raised by people of other nationalities, and a Russia inseparable from other (Western) nations.[35] The question of Russia's place vis-à-vis Western Europe was a topic of heated debate at the time, and Tur's fictional portrayal of a Russia intimately connected with Western European cultures at the personal and familial level recapitulates and intensifies arguments made by Westernizers in their debates with Slavophiles about Russia's relationship with the West and the nature of Russianness.

Antonina engages social debates in other ways as well. The novella argues (both in form and content) for a world in which connection is valued over alienation and in which the dispossessed are restored to dignity. In much the same way that Gogol "humanized" the petty government clerk, the "little man," depicting him as a human being with whom readers could have an empathic relationship, Tur recuperates another disempowered group: daughters – specifically, a governess's daughter. In so doing, Tur challenges the family as configured in Russia at midcentury. By making the daughter's discourse primary, and by portraying her as both actor and narrator, Tur rewrites familial relations and grants daughters a power and importance rare in the fiction or in the social structures of the day.[36]

The institution of the family was a vital component of the autocratic system, and, in the middle of the nineteenth century, was the focus of fierce battles to define both the family and the autocracy.[37] Daughters had the lowest status in the family (except, perhaps, for daughters-in-law).[38] At midcentury, the family was changing from an institution of primarily contractual relations to one of affective relations. In the contractual system a female child's primary importance was as a potential marriage partner (she could improve the family fortune and/or status only by marrying well); the newly emerging "affective family"[39] gave greater significance to individuals and emotions. Tur's making daughters central, then, is not merely an interesting psychological and literary stratagem, it is also an important social and political statement. Her redefinition of familial structures took place in a larger context of protest about the institution of the family: as with her presentation of nationalities, here, too, Tur represents possibilities that were under discussion by Russian liberals in other areas (such as the law). Antonina herself is an embodiment of the possibility of and the need for such social change, for after a long and painful struggle she wins the moral right to (if not the tangible reality of) an independent life. By presenting a daughter's struggle sympathetically, even empathically, Tur elaborates current social issues in fiction, and indicates the need for broader societal reform.

Tur directly attacked the Russian instantiation of the family in a review of Turgenev's third novel, *Nakanune* (*On the Eve*, 1860). She noted the need for the Russian family to change, calling it "despotic," and protested what she termed the system of "family slavery" predominant in Russia. Throughout her essay, she emphasized the difficult situation of daughters in Russian families.[40] But in the late 1840s and early 1850s, at the time she was writing *Antonina*, Tur could not yet openly discuss the need to reform the family: the system of censorship was very strict (particularly after the European revolutions of 1848) until the death of Tsar Nicholas I in 1855, and it is unlikely that she could have published direct critiques of the Russian family at this time. Instead, she addressed these issues in her fiction (e.g., *Antonina, A Mistake, Dve sestry* [*Two Sisters*], *The Niece*).[41]

Antonina reverses the powerless position of daughters by making them both the subject and the object of the narrative. And, in addition to being an account of a girl's interior growth to maturity, *Antonina* is also the tale of a daughter becoming a (step)mother.

Antonina is both stepmother to Lena, Bertini's unwanted child by a former marriage, and mother to Ida. In mothering Lena, a formerly unloved child, Antonina becomes the stepmother she wishes she had had. Tur, then, presents maternity as not mainly a matter of bearing children, but rather one of caring for them. And in her novella, motherhood is presented as closely connected to daughterhood, for Antonina's caring for Lena is a kind of wish fulfillment.

Fictional portrayals of female characters in the roles of both daughter and mother are rare; it is rarer still for the heroine to remain a central and sympathetic character in both roles, as is true of Antonina. The novella privileges female children in other ways as well: as the heroine matures, she makes her own daughters central – so much so that her relationship with her children interferes with her marriage.

Tur's focus on the mother-daughter relationship provides a curious counterpoint to many works of Western fiction in which the romantic relationship is primary.[42] The chivalric romance is not part of Russia's literary tradition, and the romance plot is not, in general, as pervasive in Russian literature as it is in Western European fiction.[43] Antonina's children become quite literally the reason that she exists: after a series of painful experiences, she contemplates suicide, but decides against it: "What would become of my daughters? They need me, they love me – this thought concentrated all my remaining energy into moving along the path of life" (143). While, given the Western and modern emphasis on individualism, Antonina's exclusive focus on her children (as the only reason to remain alive) might make today's daughters (and mothers!) cringe, in mid-nineteenth-century Russia it elevated the status of the daughter by presenting her as important, necessary.

But Antonina is not a garden-variety aristocratic daughter: she is a governess's daughter and she herself becomes a governess. This fact increases the similarity between Tur's depiction of her heroine and Pushkin's and Gogol's recovery of "the little man," for governesses, though a common feature of the aristocratic landscape, are usually mentioned only as an adjunct to the main characters; they are rarely the subject of the narrative and their psychologies are not explored. Tur shifts this emphasis throughout her tale, most explicitly when Antonina asks: "Do you know what it's like to be the daughter of a governess? It's like being everyone's Cinderella or, worse, a pariah. . . . She's obliged to please everyone, endure everything, and feel sincerely and profoundly grateful for every crumb, because she has no right to anything. . . . Endless persecution is the lot of such a child; whatever happens among the children of the family . . . she's always to blame . . . and [is] punished as an example to the rest" (11). Because Antonina has already been established as a sympathetic character, this statement comes across as a justified complaint and one that offers an imaginative entrée to the psyche of the governess's daughter, a way for readers to empathize with Antonina's sense of powerlessness.[44]

There are two other ways in which *Antonina* raises questions about the structures of the Russian family: first, in the depiction of the heroine's primary romantic attachment and her subsequent marriage (two very separate adventures), and second, in the articulation of fe/male desire. Regarding the first point: the novella recounts Antonina's and Michel's romance; from its inception, this relationship is directly connected to Antonina's father.[45] On first meeting Michel (who, as Antonina herself points out, has the same name as her father [34]), she notes: "My heart began pounding at the sound of this voice [Michel's]. It reminded me of the remote, unfamiliar resonance of my dear, kind father's voice, still alive, perpetually pleasant, stored deep within my soul" (33). She adds: "His [Michel's] voice awakened a revered memory; the color of his eyes and wavy hair revived a distant image; it seemed that in him my father was sending himself to me again" (34). The Freudian possibilities of all this are, of course, stunning, but I will leave explorations of them to other readers. Here I want to address not so much the psychosexual dynamics of Antonina's relationship with her father (although these will be implied), but rather how Antonina's search for the good father (a major theme in the novella) questions the traditional structure of the Russian family.

Antonina frequently looks back to the idyllic time when her father was alive; she describes her sense of defenselessness and need for a father's (or father substitute's) protection. Her relationships with the various men in the novella all have some element of the search for paternal protection, and all prove disappointing. Her father, while alive, offers his daughter only a limited protection; after he dies, she is left to the merciless Milkot (her stepfather); Michel, the love of her life, is totally unable to provide her with guidance or reassurance; and Bertini, the man she eventually marries, turns out to be self-absorbed and cruel. All of this suggests that a system in which a woman's well-being depends on being associated with a decent man is a faulty one. The painfully fragmented family *Antonina* presents and the reasons for that fragmentation (patriarchal authority indiscriminately exercised) is a forceful critique of the Russian family.

A second way in which Tur's novella challenges the traditional family is by candidly addressing female and male sexual desire. Until recently, it had been generally accepted that Russian fiction elides or eludes direct references to sexuality. But *Antonina* (like works by many women writers) refers explicitly to sexual passion: Bertini is sexually aggressive and Antonina submits, as she repeats over and over again, unwillingly, uncomprehendingly, out of a sense of duty, because she wants to fulfill the socially accepted role of the good wife. As we have seen in other parts of Antonina's narrative, however, submission engenders rebellion; furthermore, Antonina comes to see that Bertini's passion is not natural or even neutral. This passion is, she says, a kind of destructive selfishness, egotism, rather than being a husband's natural right as it was usually taken to be. Eventually, she feels justified in refusing his sexual demands. While Antonina's discoveries may not be startlingly new in the twentieth century, it is unusual to have such a direct articulation of the case against forced sexual relations in mid-nineteenth-century Russia.[46] And – equally important – in this discussion of conjugal relations, Antonina powerfully expresses the right of a woman to her own physical and emotional integrity and autonomy.

The heroine notes:

> The first days of our marriage remain in my memory like some confused, painful dream. His passion was alien to me; moreover, I had not a single moment of oblivion. . . . My natural timidity and my entire organism rebelled inexorably against an assertion of his rights that remained unsanctified by either warm reciprocity or the delicate sensitivity of a truly loving man. His ecstasy and rapture were alien to me – I regarded them coldly; . . . they became hateful. However, I submitted and said not a single word to let my husband know how much I suffered; I myself often attributed this feeling to inexperience. (124)

She comes to see Bertini, rather than herself, as responsible for her coldness and distance: "[Bertini's] words made a strong impression on me, forcing me to acknowledge at last how much pure egotism there was in his love for me. For the first time I didn't feel guilty for being cold to him; it occurred to me that love of that sort was merely tyranny and torment, and merited neither gratitude nor sympathy" (130).

Tur's Antonina adheres to many of the conventions of her society regarding female sexuality: the heroine repeatedly insists that she does not experience passion (124, 125) and is, in fact, repelled by Bertini's ardor. But Antonina does not reject all forms of sexual expression: she enjoys Michel's caresses (58, 124) – and finds them very different from Bertini's. While Antonina's response to her husband coincides with nineteenth-century Russian sexual mores for women, it also raises an important question: what happens to women, to marriages, when a wife submits unwillingly to her husband's sexual passion? If Antonina (or *Antonina*) is an example, the results are disastrous, both for the individuals involved and for their union. Antonina claims agency for herself as daughter, wife, and mother. In so doing, Tur's novella demands greater respect for daughters, wives, and mothers, and suggests that if the institution of the family is to survive, it must be radically transformed. It is unclear whether Tur consciously set out to question the permanence of familial structures, but her novella enacts a serious challenge to them, for Antonina creates a new kind of family based on her relationship with her daughters, a family of women and one based on mutual affection and respect rather than on traditional structures of authority.[47]

》 《

One episode in Tur's life has particular resonance for reading *Antonina*. Like her heroine, Tur planned to elope (with her tutor, Nikolai Nadezhdin) but, at the last moment, the elopement did not occur. Tur and Nadezhdin were intensely involved with one another in 1834 and 1835 (their impassioned correspondence runs to more than eight hundred pages), but the relationship was equally intensely opposed by Tur's family, who did not want their daughter marrying a "seminarist," someone of the lower clerical estate.[48] Eventually, the two decided to elope, but Tur arrived late and, according to Aleksandr Herzen, Nadezhdin unromantically fell asleep while waiting for her, and the marriage never took place. The failed elopement in *Antonina* is very different from Tur's experience with Nadezhdin, for it is Antonina who – in response to a letter from Michel's aunt – decides to call it off.[49] Is this rewriting, then, a form of literary revenge? Is Tur rewriting her own elopement in *Antonina*, giving the heroine greater control?

The question of how an author's works and life are or may be related (in all senses) is an important one. Works by women have often been read as simple extensions or descriptions of their lives rather than as artistic (re)creations. In the case of Tur, scholars have generally assumed that the events depicted in her fiction can be explained (away) by the events of her biography.[50] This approach (intentionally or not) serves to devalue Tur's skill and talent; it also assumes an unproblematic link between "literature" and "life."[51] Therefore, while acknowledging the complex interplay of life and works, it is particularly important to question this easy equation of women's lives and their fictions and, so, the erasure of women's artistry. Tur, like male authors, certainly draws upon her lived experience in her fiction, but we cannot know the complicated processes that turn that experience into representation, nor can we assume a one-to-one correspondence between the text of Tur's life and that of her fiction.

》 《

Antonina is written mainly in the language of sentiment; as a result, it may be considered inartistic and simplistic by many late twentieth-century readers.[52] But a close reading of the novella reveals many complexities in the construction of the text: for example, *Antonina* establishes a series of relationships with Tur's other works, thus creating an open-ended fiction and raising still more questions about the interrelations of "life" and "literature"; the novella also elaborates what I will call an aesthetic of communication.

The very form in which *Antonina* was published pushes the boundaries of the text and of (inter)textuality. *Antonina* appeared separately as "An Episode from a Novel" early in 1851; later that year it was published as volume 3 of Tur's novel *The Niece*. Antonina's story was also continued in *Two Sisters* (1851), a novella about Antonina's daughters, who recount parts of their mother's story. This publishing history raises many questions: Can *Antonina* stand on its own as a text? Is it a fragment?[53] What are we to make of *Two Sisters*, which is "not quite a sequel" to this "not quite a novella"?[54] And how is *Antonina* related to Tur's larger work, *The Niece?*

One way in which *Antonina* is connected to *The Niece* is in the (sometimes confusing) style of narration: Antonina frequently breaks off her tale and makes direct reference to her hearers and friends, Pletneev, Ilmenev, and Masha. These are characters from the larger narrative, *The Niece,* with whom the reader of the novel is familiar by volume 3, but whom the reader of *Antonina* will not recognize. For the latter, the heroine's frequent references to unknown characters suggest a continuation of life beyond the immediate work, thus blurring the boundary between written text and lived experience. In fact, the boundaries between narratives of all sorts (written, oral, lived) nearly dissolve in *Antonina.*

This interactive narration also stresses the act of communication which, together with the closely related concept of community, is central in *Antonina.* Antonina is isolated throughout the work, both because of her social position and the deliberate actions of her stepparents, who try to keep her away from others. But even though all the usual relationships (romance, marriage, relations with parents and stepparents) break down, several alternative communities are established in and beyond the novella: between Antonina and her two daughters; between Antonina and other characters in the novella; between Antonina and other characters in *The Niece;* between Antonina and the characters in the later *Two Sisters;* and between *Antonina* and its readers. In the novella itself, Antonina is left with a few intense attachments: she is deeply devoted to her daughters and Madame Beillant. Furthermore, one of those who listens to Antonina's tale in volume 3 (Pletneev) later becomes her husband in *The Niece.* And these relations of community are extensive: contemporary readers describe a deep, even passionate empathy with the character of Antonina.[55] Despite (or perhaps because of) a great many odds, the heroine manages to form several alternative communities in the novella itself, as well as in the larger novel, and beyond (her daughters, her hearers, and sympathetic readers). These communities are emphasized throughout the novella, as is the act of communication or narration, which is presented as the way to attain community; this focus stands in stark contrast to the isolation presented in much Russian literature of the time.[56]

Narration, in this novella, also seduces: Pletneev marries Antonina as a direct result of hearing her story. In modeling the ability of narrative to affect characters' lives powerfully, Tur again valorizes communication as the force that breaks down old patterns and establishes new relationships and new communities. In this way, too, *Antonina* is a work with a social message: to present the power of narration and to represent the possibility and desirability of new forms of community was potentially subversive, especially during the reign of Nicholas I (1825–55). Thus, *Antonina*'s aesthetic of fluidity, community, and communication works on both the social and artistic levels, which are, if not inseparable, then closely intertwined throughout the novella.

》 《

By presenting daughters as important, privileging a wife's desire over her husband's, and depicting the emotional bonds between mothers and daughters as primary, as an alternative – and a better (if still imperfect) – approach to family, Tur's novella challenges the traditional structures of the Russian family; *Antonina*, then, clearly addresses social issues. But it is also a work with an intriguing aesthetic, one in which orality and an emphasis on communication combine to extend the boundaries of the text. *Antonina* is one – of many – examples of Russian women's writings at midcentury that serve to complicate common understandings not only of women's writing in Russia, but also of the Russian literary tradition more broadly: that tradition is even richer – more extensive and complex – than has usually been thought or taught.

Tur was a writer, critic, editor of a journal, and *salonière;* her effect on the field of Russian letters was profound.[57] Her novella

Antonina was the sensation of the year (1851) in Russia's literary circles; it gained its power and renown, I have argued, both through its social critique and its eloquent aesthetic. Now, nearly 150 years later, it is appearing in English for the first time. How, I wonder, will it be understood in these new contexts?

I would like to thank Sibelan Forrester, Michael Katz, Susan Larsen, Katherine Morrissey, and Barbara Norton for insightful, incisive, and thought-provoking comments on earlier versions of this manuscript. Special thanks are due to Mary Zirin for the many ways she has contributed to this project.

1. "Evgeniya Tur," née Sukhovo-Kobylina, was by marriage the Countess Elizaveta Salias de Turnemir (Sailhas de Tournemire).

2. See, e.g., Nikolai Knizhnik [Golitsyn], *Slovar' russkikh pisatel'nits, 1759–1859, Russkii arkhiv* 11–12 (1865): 1205; I. S. Turgenev, *Polnoe sobranie sochinenii i pisem,* 30 vols. (Moscow: Nauka, 1978–90), 4:473–90; A. N. Ostrovsky, "Oshibka," in *Polnoe sobranie sochinenii,* 12 vols. (Moscow: Iskusstvo, 1978), 10:7–17.

3. An initial enthusiastic critical response followed by a much cooler response is a typical pattern of reception for works by Russian women prose authors of the period (e.g., Nadezhda Durova, Karolina Pavlova). On the reception of works by women poets, see Diana Greene, "Nineteenth-Century Women Poets: Critical Reception vs. Self-Definition," in *Women in Russian Literature,* ed. Toby W. Clyman and Diana Greene (Westport, Conn.: Praeger, 1994), 95–109.

4. *Russian Speech* ran out of funds in 1862 and had to be closed (many journals of this period had similarly short runs). "Aesthetic" critics (e.g., P. V. Annenkov) considered artistry primary, while

"radical" critics (e.g., N. G. Chernyshevsky) emphasized the social function of art. The Slavophiles (roughly, those who looked to Russian and, more broadly, Slavic traditions for cultural, political, religious, and/or social models) and Westernizers (those who believed that Russia must incorporate Western European mores and models) engaged in important debates throughout the nineteenth century, beginning in the late 1830s. These debates continue in different forms to the present day.

5. Although it is now clear that many more women than have been suspected were involved in fiction, criticism, and journalism, women ran into many obstacles in such attempts (both financial and attitudinal). See, e.g., Carolyn Marks, "'Provid[ing] Amusement for the Ladies': The Creation of the Russian Women's Magazine in the 1880s," forthcoming in a collection of essays on women and journalism in Imperial Russia, ed. Jehanne Gheith and Barbara Norton (Durham, N.C.: Duke University Press), and Rhonda Lebedev Clark, "Claiming Voice, Profession, Livelihood: Women Periodical Publishers and Editors of Moscow and St. Petersburg, 1860–1905," unpublished ms.

6. See D. D. Yazykov, *Obzor zhizni i trudov pokoinikh russkikh pisatelei i pisatel'nits* (St. Petersburg: Akademiya nauk, 1912), 12:172–73. Gippius (Hippius) refers to Tur's novel *Plemyannitsa* (*The Niece*) in "Outside of Time: An Old Etude," in *A Russian Cultural Revival: A Critical Anthology of Emigré Literature before 1939,* ed. and trans. Temira Pachmuss (Knoxville: University of Tennessee Press, 1981), 40; Tsvetaeva refers to Tur's work in her autobiographical prose work "The Devil," in *A Captive Spirit: Selected Prose,* ed. and trans. J. Marin King (Ann Arbor, Mich.: Ardis, 1980), 191. My thanks to Judith Kalb for the reference to Gippius.

7. Turgenev, *Polnoe sobranie sochinenii i pisem,* 4:486 (see excerpt in this volume, pp. 149–51).

8. "Kometa. Ucheno-literaturnyi al'manakh, izdannyi Nikolaem Shchepkinym," *Otechestvennye zapiski* 76, no. 5 (1851): 1–28, esp. 25; "Kometa. Ucheno-literaturnyi al'manakh, izdannyi Nikolaem Shchepkinym," *Sovremennik* 27, no. 5 (May 1851): 1–32, esp. 2, 4; A. Grigor'ev, "Russkaya literatura v 1851 godu," 4th and final article, *Moskvityanin*, no. 4 (February 1852): 95–108, esp. 98–99.

9. The collections edited by N. Yakushin and V. Uchenova are exceptions. Uchenova includes nothing by Tur; Yakushin includes Tur's "Dolg" ("Duty"). See N. Yakushin, *"Serdtsa chutkogo prozren'em . . . ": Povesti i rasskazy russkikh pisatel'nits XIX v.* (Moscow: Sovetskaya Rossiya, 1991); and V. Uchenova, *Dacha na Petergofskom doroge: Proza russkikh pisatel'nits pervoi poloviny XIX veka* (Moscow: Sovremennik, 1986), *Svidanie: Proza russkikh pisatel'nits 60–80x godov XIX veka* (Moscow: Sovremennik, 1987), and *Tol'ko chas: Proza russkikh pisatel'nits kontsa XIX–nachala XX veka* (Moscow: Sovremennik, 1988).

10. The recent publication of Joe Andrew's fine volume of translations has significantly increased the number of nineteenth-century prose fictions by Russian women available in English. See Joe Andrew, trans., *Russian Women's Shorter Fiction: An Anthology, 1835–1860* (Oxford: Clarendon Press, 1996). Even with this volume, however, the work accessible in English translation represents a very small portion of the rich body of Russian women's writings. In addition to Andrew's volume, works of prose fiction by nineteenth-century Russian women in English translation that are currently in print or widely available in U.S. university libraries are: Karolina Pavlova's *A Double Life* (*Dvoinaya zhizn'*, 1848), trans. Barbara Heldt, 3d ed. (Oakland, Calif.: Barbary Coast Books, 1996); Evdokiya Rostopchina's *Rank and Money* (*Chiny i den'gi*, 1839), trans. and ed. Helena Goscilo, in *Russian and Polish Women's Fiction* (Knoxville: University of Tennessee Press, 1985), 44–84; and two selections in Catriona Kelly's *Anthology of Russian Women's*

Writing (Pavlova's 1859 *At the Tea Table* and Sof'ya Soboleva's 1863 *Pros and Cons*). Some Russian women's autobiographical writings of the period are available in English translation, though still relatively few.

11. The processes by which nineteenth-century Russian women authors have been forgotten have begun to be explored by a number of scholars. See, e.g., the articles by Jane Costlow, Diana Greene, and Mary Zirin in Clyman and Greene, eds., *Women in Russian Literature;* Jehanne Gheith, "In Her Own Voice: Evgeniya Tur, Author, Critic, Journalist" (Ph.D. diss., Stanford University, 1992); Barbara Heldt, *Terrible Perfection* (Bloomington: Indiana University Press, 1987); and Catriona Kelly, *A History of Russian Women's Writing: 1820–1992* (Oxford: Clarendon Press, 1994).

12. It may seem that I am claiming a great deal by using the term "women's writing" rather than a narrower phrase (e.g., "prose fiction"). I have deliberately kept the term broad, for these women's works include poetry, prose, autobiographical writings, literary criticism, and publicistics (a kind of social commentary common in Russian journalism). Although I examine only fiction in this essay, I hope that women's writings in all their variety will be studied in greater depth than they have been to date.

13. Elena Andreevna Gan, born Fadeeva (1814–42), was widely considered one of the leading woman writers in Russia; she published under the pseudonym Zeneida R——va. Anna Vasil'evna Korvin-Krukovskaya (married name, Jaclard) was born in 1843 and died in 1887. Sister of the mathematician and author Sof'ya Kovalevskaya, Korvin-Krukovskaya published in the 1860s in the Dostoevsky brothers' journal *Epokha* (*The Epoch*). Avdot'ya Yakovleva Panaeva, née Brianskaya (1819/20–93), published under the name of N. Stanitsky. She was the wife of the writer Ivan Panaev, who, with Nikolai Nekrasov, edited the journal *Sovremennik* from 1847 until Panaev's death in 1862.

14. Nadezhda Durova (1783–1866), who published many works of fiction, is best known as the author of *The Cavalry Maiden,* ed. and trans. Mary Zirin (Bloomington: Indiana University Press, 1988); Evdokiya Rostopchina (1811–58) was a poet and prose author; Karolina Pavlova (1807–93), a poet and author of prose fiction, including *A Double Life;* of the three Khvoshchinskaya sisters, Nadezhda (1820?–89), Sof'ya (1828?–65), and Praskov'ya (183?–1916), Nadezhda (V. Krestovsky, pseud.) was the most prolific; both she and Sof'ya wrote biting satires of Russian provincial life.

15. The "superfluous man" is a common literary character and a defining cultural and social figure in Russian literature: see, e.g., Turgenev's *Rudin,* Pushkin's *Evgeny Onegin,* Lermontov's Pechorin in *A Hero of Our Time,* and Goncharov's *Oblomov;* see also the criticism on the topic, notably N. A. Dobrolyubov, "When Will the Day Come?" (1860), in *Selected Philosophical Essays,* trans. J. Fineberg (Moscow: Foreign Languages Publishing House, 1956), 389–441.

16. Tur to Turgenev, winter 1850, Institut Russkoi literatury, St. Petersburg (hereafter IRLI), Papers of I. S. Turgenev, 5850.xxxb 140, l. 2.

17. Turgenev, letters of November and December 1850, *Polnoe sobranie sochinenii i pisem, Pis'ma,* 2:74, 75.

18. Jane Costlow, "Speaking the Sorrow of Women: Turgenev's 'Neschastnaia' and Evgeniia Tur's 'Antonina,'" *Slavic Review* (Summer 1991): 328–35. For a fuller discussion of the interrelationship of Tur's *Antonina* and Turgenev's *Diary,* see my "The Superfluous Man and the Necessary Woman: A 'Re-vision,'" *Russian Review* (April 1996): 226–44.

19. This review of *Plemyannitsa* is the same essay quoted above and is excerpted at the end of this volume. It was originally published in *Sovremennik,* no. 1 (January 1852): 1–14.

20. Turgenev, *Polnoe sobranie sochinenii i pisem*, 4:477.

21. Ibid., 4:479.

22. While the term "automatically secondary" is my own, there is a great deal of scholarship that argues convincingly that women's writing has been considered of lesser value than men's (in various cultural contexts). A few examples from this enormous body of literature are: Nina Baym, *Women's Fiction: A Guide to Novels by and about Women in America, 1820–1870* (Ithaca, N.Y.: Cornell University Press, 1978); Sandra M. Gilbert and Susan Gubar, *The Madwoman in the Attic* (New Haven, Conn.: Yale University Press, 1979); Catriona Kelly, *A History of Russian Women's Writing, 1820–1992*; Susie Tharu and K. Lalita, eds., *Women's Writing in India, 600 B.C. to the Present*, 2 vols. (New York: Feminist Press, 1991), see esp. their introduction, 1:1–37; and Dale Spender, *The Writing or the Sex?* (New York: Pergamon Press, 1989).

23. On the devaluation of the feminine in recent Russian writing, see Helena Goscilo, "*Domostroika* or *Perestroika?* The Construction of Womanhood in Soviet Culture under Glasnost," in *Late Soviet Culture from Perestroika to Novostroika*, ed. Thomas Lahusen with Gene Kuperman (Durham, N.C.: Duke University Press, 1993), 233–55. See also Goscilo, ed., *Skirted Issues: The Discreteness and Indiscretions of Russian Women's Prose*, *Russian Studies in Literature*, vol. 28 (Armonk, N.Y.: M. E. Sharpe, 1992).

24. See, e.g., V. G. Belinsky, "Povesti Mar'i Zhukovoi" (1840), in *Sobranie sochinenii* (Moscow: Khudozhestvennaya literatura, 1978); N. A. Nekrasov, "Zametki o zhurnalakh. Mart. 1856 goda," in *Polnoe sobranie sochinenii i pisem* (Moscow: GIZ, 1950), 9:390–405; A. N. Ostrovsky, "Oshibka" (n. 2 above); and N. V. Shelgunov, "Zhenskoe bezdushie," *Delo* 9 (1870): 11.

25. See, e.g., the entries on Tur in Yazykov, *Obzor zhizni i trudov russkikh pisatelei i pisatel'nits* (n. 6 above), 12:167; A. A. Surkov et

al., eds., *Kratkaya literaturnaya entsiklopediya* (Moscow: Sovetskaya entsiklopediya, 1972), 655–56; and Victor Terras, ed., *Handbook of Russian Literature* (New Haven, Conn.: Yale University Press, 1985), 487–88.

26. Konstantin Bestuzhev-Ryumin was actively engaged in improving women's position in Russia: the Bestuzhev Higher Courses for Women were (later) named after him.

27. Tur to Konstantin Bestuzhev-Ryumin, mid-January 1852, IRLI, Papers of K. N. Bestuzhev-Ryumin, 25.164, ll. 85–87.

28. Tur was still troubled by this review more than a year after it appeared. See Tur to Turgenev, April 1853, IRLI, Papers of I. S. Turgenev, 5850.xxxb 140, l. 68.

29. I do not want to make too sharp a division here, for many women did publish critical articles and many men wrote literary critiques in personal correspondence. But while the letters of many male authors are easily available in their collected works, letters by women, in most cases, are available only in archives or occasionally in prerevolutionary journals.

30. See Tur's letters to her family, Rossiiskaya gosudarstvennaya biblioteka, Moscow, MS Division, fond 223, and to I. S. Turgenev, IRLI, Papers of I. S. Turgenev, 5850.xxxb 140, and N. D. Khvoshchinskaya's letters to A. A. Kraevsky, Saltykov-Shchedrin Library, MS Division, fond 391, delo 803, as well as the excerpts from her letters in three articles entitled "N. D. Khvoshchinskaya-Zaionchkovskaya (V. Krestovsky – psevdonim)" by V. Semevsky in *Russkaya mysl'*, October–December 1890.

31. While I am aware of the mutual influence of the "social" and the "literary" or "artistic," I have tried not to conflate these realms; this separation is particularly important to maintain in Russian contexts in which, for a very long time, the "social" and the "literary" have been explicitly intertwined, sometimes to the point of identifi-

cation.

32. Tur explicitly connects *Antonina* and *Jane Eyre* by naming Antonina's stepfather Milkot after Millcote, the name of the town near which Rochester's estate is located. I am grateful to Svetlana Grenier for pointing this out. Also, Tur later published an article on the Brontës: "Miss Bronte, ee zhizn' i sochineniya," *Russkii vestnik* 6 (1859): 461–500.

33. The Russian system of estates is difficult to define. As Gregory Freeze notes: "The Russian *soslovie* represented something more than a European estate but less than a formal caste." See Freeze, "Caste and Emancipation: The Changing Status of Clerical Families in the Great Reforms," in *The Family in Imperial Russia,* ed. David Ransel (Urbana: University of Illinois Press, 1978), 124–50, quote on 124.

34. "Kometa," *Otechestvennye zapiski* (n. 8 above), 27, 28.

35. The question of Russia's relationship to the "West" is extremely complicated; Russia (like Spain) is part of what might be called the "peripheral West" – sometimes it is considered part of the West and sometimes not.

36. Although there are many autobiographies of Russian daughters (e.g., Panaeva's fictionalized *Semeistvo Tal'nikovykh* and works by Durova and Kovalevskaya), there is little known fiction in which daughters are the primary focus (Pavlova's *A Double Life* is one exception). Pushkin's *Evgeny Onegin* (1831), Herzen's *Kto vinovat? (Who Is to Blame?* 1847), and Turgenev's *Nakanune (On the Eve,* 1860) all detail the development of women-who-are-daughters, but in these cases the female character's role as daughter is not the primary emphasis, as it is in *Antonina.* Increasingly, female-authored fictions focusing on daughters are being discovered, so that we may find that these were much more common than has previously been thought.

37. William G. Wagner, *Marriage, Property and Law in Late*

Imperial Russia (Oxford: Clarendon Press, 1994).

38. On the position of daughters (in-law) in Russia in the nineteenth century, see Beatrice Farnsworth, "The Litigious Daughter-in-Law," *Slavic Review* 45 (Spring 1986): 49–64; and Evgeniya Tur, "Vospominaniya i razmyshleniya," *Vremya* 10, no. 6 (June 1862): 45–67. See also Sibelan Forrester's translation of Tur's article, "Reflections and Ruminations"; it is available on the AWSS Web page: <http:///ash.swarthmore.edu/slavic/turr&r.html>.

39. Here I use William Wagner's terminology (see Wagner, *Marriage, Property and Law*).

40. Evgeniya Tur, "A Few Words Regarding 'The Russian Woman's' Article, 'Elena Nikolaevna Stakhova,'" *Moskovskie vedomosti*, no. 85 (17 April 1860): 665–67. Excerpts from this essay will appear in English translation in Robin Bisha, Jehanne Gheith, Christine Holden, Barbara Norton, and William G. Wagner, eds., *Russian Women: Experience and Expression: An Anthology of Sources* (Bloomington: Indiana University Press, forthcoming). On the position of daughters in Russian society, see also Tur, "Vospominaniya i razmyshleniya" (n. 38 above), 53–54.

41. *Oshibka* was published in 1849; the other works were published in 1851.

42. Karolina Pavlova in *A Double Life* also emphasizes the mother-daughter relationship (as well as unhappy marriages).

43. "Western Europe" is a term with many meanings; I use it to designate England, France, Germany, and sometimes the United States. There is an enormous body of scholarship that details the importance of the romance plot in Western European literatures. The following are works that I have found particularly helpful: Marianne Hirsch, *The Mother/Daughter Plot: Narrative, Psychoanalysis, Feminism* (Bloomington: Indiana University Press, 1989); Judith Lowder Newton, *Women, Power, and Subversion: Social Strategies in British Fiction, 1778–1860* (Athens: University of Georgia Press,

1981); and Janice A. Radway, *Reading the Romance: Women, Patriarchy, and Popular Literature,* 2d ed. (Chapel Hill: University of North Carolina Press, 1991).

44. While the role of the governess has been relatively little discussed by scholars of Russian history or Russian literature, "governess literature" has proven to be an extremely fruitful area of inquiry for literary scholars – and historians – of Britain. Russian exemplars, too, should be studied in depth. Tur's later *Zakoldovannyi krug (An Enchanted Circle)* is another example of "governess literature" (*Zakoldovannyi krug, Otechestvennye zapiski* 1–2 [January/February 1854]: 139–204). For the British case, see, e.g., M. Jeanne Peterson, "The Victorian Governess: Status Incongruence in Family and Society," in *Suffer and Be Still: Women in the Victorian Age,* ed. Martha Vicinus (Bloomington: Indiana University Press, 1972), 3–19; and Mary Poovey, *Uneven Developments: The Ideological Working of Gender in Mid-Victorian England* (Chicago: University of Chicago Press, 1988).

45. On fictional relationships between fathers and daughters as well as the relationship of the writing daughter and her father in Western contexts, see Lynda Zwinger, *Daughters, Fathers, and the Novel: The Sentimental Romance of Heterosexuality* (Madison: University of Wisconsin Press, 1991). For Russian examples, see Nadezhda Durova's portrayal of her father and father figures in *The Cavalry Maiden,* and Beth Holmgren, "Why Russian Girls Loved Charskaya," *Russian Review* (January 1995), esp. 101, 102–3.

46. By the 1870s and 1880s there was a great deal of writing against forced sexual relations, but *Antonina* is early, unusually explicit, and psychologically accurate. I am grateful to Mary Zirin for the information about the 1870s and 1880s, and for clarifying my thinking on this point.

47. It is interesting that the effectiveness of this new kind of fam-

ily is called into question both in *Antonina* itself and in the later *Two Sisters*. In the former work, Antonina, while professing the most intense love for her daughters, leaves them for two years. It is possible to read this also as a critique of patriarchal authority (Bertini comes between Antonina and her daughters, and she has no legal right to resist).

48. The correspondence between Nadezhdin and Tur is housed at IRLI (25.494, 25.495, and fond 199, op. 2, dela 47, 49). Parts of it have been published in N. K. Kozmin, ed., "Nikolai Ivanovich Nadezhdin. Zhizn' i nauchno-literaturnaya deyatel'nost', 1804–1836," *Zapiski istoriko-filologicheskogo fakul'teta* (1912), chast' 111, 457–506.

49. In the novella, Michel's aunt is partly responsible for the failed elopement, as Antonina makes her decision not to run away with Michel only when she understands that his aunt will never forgive him for marrying Antonina; still, this is a very different situation from having one's intended drowse off while waiting for the beloved to appear.

50. Examples of this narrowly biographical approach include Leonid Grossman, *Prestuplenie Sukhovo-Kobylina* (1928; facsimile, Ann Arbor, Mich.: University Microfilms International, 1978); Viktor Grossman, *Delo Sukhovo-Kobylina* (Moscow: Khudozhestvennaya literatura, 1936); and B. Koz'min, ed., "Pis'ma Ogareva k E. V. Salias de Turnemir," *Literaturnoe nasledstvo* (1953), 61:797–844.

51. The complexities of the relationship(s) between "literature" and "life" in the Russian context (though in an earlier period) have been elegantly detailed by William Mills Todd III in "*Eugene Onegin:* 'Life's Novel,'" in *Literature and Society in Imperial Russia, 1800–1914,* ed. William Mills Todd III (Stanford, Calif.: Stanford University Press, 1978), 203–35.

52. My line of argument in this section owes a great deal to Jane

Tompkins's discussion of *Uncle Tom's Cabin.* See Tompkins, *Sensational Designs: The Cultural Work of American Fiction, 1790–1860* (New York: Oxford University Press, 1985), 122–46.

53. For a splendid discussion of the importance of the fragment in Russian literature of a slightly earlier period, see Monika Greenleaf, *Pushkin and Romantic Fashion: Fragment, Elegy, Orient, Irony* (Stanford, Calif.: Stanford University Press, 1994).

54. A further twist to this intertextual medley is that Tur essentially repeats the plot of *Two Sisters* in *An Enchanted Circle,* but radically revises the ending.

55. See, for example, "Kometa," *Sovremennik* (n. 8 above), 2; "Kometa," *Otechestvennye zapiski* (n. 8 above), 25–26; Turgenev, *Polnoe sobranie sochinenii i pisem,* 4:486–87.

56. I am thinking in particular of the literature in which the superfluous man figures (from Onegin to Rudin). While he may be eloquent, the superfluous man is unable to communicate or to establish lasting connections with others (excepting, perhaps, his readers).

57. On Tur's importance for Russian letters, see A. S. Dolinin's introduction to A. P. Suslova, *Gody blizosti s Dostoevskim* (Moscow: Iskra revolyutsii, 1928), and the many reviews of Tur's works (for these and related references, see my dissertation [n. 11 above], 213–34).

»»» TRANSLATOR'S NOTE «««

Evgeniya Tur's four-volume novel *Plemyannitsa* (*The Niece*) was published in Moscow in 1851. One section of that work was originally published under the title *Antonina* in the almanac *Kometa* (*The Comet*), edited by Nikolai Shchepkin (Moscow, 1851). The text for this translation was taken from volume 3 of the four-volume novel.

The system of transliteration is that used in the *Oxford Slavonic Papers*, with the following exceptions: hard and soft signs have been omitted and conventional spellings of names have been retained.

I wish to express my gratitude to the University Research Institute at the University of Texas at Austin for a Special Research Grant to complete this project.

Special thanks are due to William Mills Todd at Harvard, who first drew my attention to the work; to Jehanne Gheith at Duke, who supplied me with the text and encouraged me at every stage; and to Mary Zirin, whose suggestions and corrections were invaluable. I am also grateful to my faithful research assistant, Ryan Phelps, and my excellent "in-house" editor and proofreader, Sally Furgeson.

»»» LIST OF CHARACTERS «««

Antonína Mikháilovna Stein (Nína, Nínochka)	*the heroine*
Adele	*her mother*
Papa	*her father*
Madame Stein	*her stepmother*
Milkót	*her stepfather*
The Vélins	*Antonina's neighbors*
Natálya Andréevna	
Kátya (Kátenka, Catherine)	*her eldest daughter*
The Chernetsóvs	*Antonina's employers*
Iván Sídorovich	
Glafíra Vasílevna	*his wife*
Várya (Várinka)	*their daughter*
Sásha (Sashúr)	*their son*
Madame Beillant	*a young French widow, a friend of Antonina's father*
Mikhaíl Arkádich B** (Michel)	*the "hero"*
Dmítry Z**	*his friend*
Vasíly N** (Vásya)	*another friend*
Albert Bertini	*an Italian businessman*
Léna (Lénochka)	*his daughter from a previous marriage*
Ída (Ídochka)	*his and Antonina's daughter*

»»» «««
Antonina

>»» «««
Antonina
An Episode from a Novel

I don't remember my early childhood; I only know that I was born in Mainz* and taken to Russia at the age of three. Since that time I can recall the first moments of my life as if in a dream, where the image of my father always appears before my eyes. I will try to convey my vague recollections. At first I remember him as a young, fair-haired, handsome man with a clear gaze and a pleasant voice. It's as if I can hear him now, when he used to call me, sit me on his lap, and play with my hair, which was fair and wavy just like his. I recall how he would often say, addressing my mother:

"Adele! Our Ninochka* looks just like me; only her eyes are neither yours nor mine. . . . Whose eyes does she have? What magnificent eyes!"

And he would set about kissing me; he often spent the whole evening playing with me, sitting on my little rug strewn with toys. My father seems to have been fairly well-off and lived a comfortable life. Subsequently, everything changed. He became a widower and a year later married a young Parisian woman who charmed him with her beauty and kindness. The first years of this marriage were apparently happy; I was so little I can't tell you much about this period. Then my memory becomes confused; I don't know many details about what happened to my father: later I was told he suffered losses in unsuccessful commercial transactions; he was forced to abandon his position and become a private tutor of German, while my stepmother became a governess in the same household. I remember him as sickly and gloomy at that time.

Clear recollections of my childhood begin on one long winter evening. Just as now, I see myself in a large, cold, towering room; it's dark all around me; a bright fireplace stands along one side; a dim candle burns in the corner. The glow of the fire, red and flickering, flares up and dies down, at times brightly illuminating objects in the room, casting their long, pale shadows on the lacquered parquet. Ancient portraits on the walls stare sternly from their darkened, once-gilded frames; in the clear reflection of the flames, they exert a powerful grip on my childish sensibility and frighten me. I sit cowering in one corner of the room, completely alone – I'm cold and afraid. My shoulders and hands are exposed; the fireplace draws me invitingly and irresistibly – I look around, there's no one in the room, so I get up timidly and approach the flames. Once again glancing around fearfully, I make sure that I'm really alone, the doors are closed, and no one else is in the room. Then I grow bolder and move toward the blazing fireplace, stretching my icy hands to the flames; gradually, life-giving warmth flows into me. I sit down on a little bench that has been left next to the fire and sink into a reverie – far off, like an echo, I hear loud shouting and children running in the next room; my stepmother is with them. She can't leave them alone, so I'm completely safe. Then I surrender entirely to the pleasure of physical well-being; a book lies on my lap, my hands folded on it, but my eyes are fixed on the fire and follow the flickering flames, their bending and curling. Suddenly, a harsh, robust voice resounds behind me:

"Who let you sit by the fireplace? Your mama forbids you to be anywhere near it."

I shudder and turn around. Milkot* is standing right behind me.

"Come on. I'll take you to Madame Stein," he says. Grabbing

hold of my hand, he leads me to the door, opens it, and takes me into the drawing room.

The children were playing their favorite game, stagecoach. Numerous chairs were gathered together; one of the children sat up front and acted as coachman; the rest were seated behind in pairs and pretended to be different families, equipped with their dolls and toys; each child took charge of two or three chairs. As soon as Milkot entered the room, leading me by the hand, the children fell silent; the coachman ceased waving his rope, whipping the four chairs representing fantastic horses; they all turned toward me with cold and proud curiosity rather than indifference. My stepmother was sitting in the corner and also glanced up at us; her work dropped slowly to her knees. Milkot led me to her and said:

"Madame Stein, I caught Antonina next to the fireplace. I know you don't allow her to go anywhere near it, so I brought her in here to you."

"Why were you sitting near the fireplace?" my stepmother asked, looking at me sternly.

I remained silent.

"Why did you go near the fireplace, I'm asking you?"

"It was cold in that room," I said. "My dress has a low neck. I was freezing."

"Do I allow you to sit near the fire?"

I was silent, knowing that excuses were to no avail. She took me by the hand and led me to her own room; my father was sitting there reading. She shoved me into a small, dark closet filled with dresses and locked me in. I sat in silence, covering myself with dresses because I felt so cold. From there I could hear the conversation between my father and stepmother: first, only muffled sounds reached me; then, as their voices grew louder, each word came through clearly and was etched deeply in my memory.

"You despise her," my father said. "What for? Is it because she looks like me? Is it because you no longer love me and now love someone else? Wait a little while; have patience; I'll die soon and you'll be free."

"When will you stop your raving?" my stepmother said to him and walked out of the room.

My father came up to the closet, opened it, and, not seeing me, called tenderly:

"Ninochka, where are you?"

"Here I am, Papa," I said, sticking my head out from behind some dresses.

He took me by the hand and helped me out of the closet, sat me down, and asked me why I was being punished. When I started to tell him and mentioned the name Milkot, he seemed to make an involuntary gesture – but didn't say anything. Stroking my head, he merely talked to me for a long time, asking me to be meek, obedient, and submissive.

I listened to him carefully, but even more I looked at him and examined his face with timid love. Struck by his reference to death in the conversation with my stepmother, I noticed for the first time his listless face where the destructive hand of time, or more likely, illness, had left its heavy imprint. He was pale, his cheeks were sunken, he was extremely gaunt, and his blue eyes shone with unusual brightness. He looked at me for a while and at long last a large tear dropped slowly and quietly from his cheek onto my head. I embraced him and burst into tears. I was still pressed against his chest, my arms embracing his neck, when footsteps in the next room could be heard coming toward us. He suddenly made an anxious and involuntary movement, which I understood; I jumped quickly off his lap and rushed back into the closet. As I was hurrying to get in, I happened to turn around and, in a moment, my glance took in the whole room: my father stood there, his face flushed and burning bright red. I closed the door at once, but took that impression into the closet with me; his image, like a vision, was engraved in my memory so deeply that I can still recall that moment very clearly. I don't know if it was my father's awareness of his own weakness that made him caress his daughter in secret from his wife or shame at being so well understood by a child and disgust with himself. At almost the same time my stepmother entered the room, he approached the closet, opened the door, and, as he let me out, he instructed:

"Ninochka, go to your mother, ask her forgiveness, and promise that you won't disobey her in the future."

I timidly left my captivity, but after glancing at my stepmother's cold, severe expression, I didn't dare take a single step and stopped.

"Forgive her," he urged my stepmother coldly. "She won't disobey you anymore."

"There's no need for me to forgive her," said my stepmother. "You seem to have done so already."

"Forgive her," he said in irritation. "Do you hear? Nina, kiss your mother's hand."

I went up to her. Without looking at me she extended her hand. I kissed it coldly, only for show, feeling disgust with her and myself that I had to appear so submissive.

"Go and play," my father said to me. "Join the other children!"

I left the room and went into the drawing room.

Don't chastise me for describing my childhood in such detail; subsequently you'll see that all the seeds of my future unhappiness are contained within it. I don't know if I've said that at the time we were staying in the house of a wealthy landowner, Mr. Velin, on his large estate far from Moscow. Milkot was an Englishman living there as a tutor. In general, relations between my father and stepmother had obviously changed since Milkot had become acquainted with them and grown so close to my stepmother, which was only natural since they lived in the same house and worked together. Permit me not to go into detail about all this; I'll merely state that at first my father was jealous of my stepmother's affection for Milkot. Later he distanced himself from her, became very cool with her, gloomy with everyone else, and began to despise Milkot; with each passing day his health deteriorated. As for me, I don't know how and why I became the object of Milkot's extreme dislike; since then I've thought long and hard about the past and have come to the conclusion that, not without cause, I may have been the innocent party who opened my father's eyes and forced him to confront Milkot's love for my stepmother. I loved my father passionately; perhaps my childish chatter and innumerable stories led him to discover the truth and compelled him to understand. Whatever the case, Milkot despised me, and my stepmother was cold and implacably stern with me; my father's interference in our relations merely inflamed her more against me and did me harm, leading to new punishments, one after another. If I was rescued from one of them by my father, I had to expect to incur another harsher punishment immediately. I don't know whether it was pure chance or my stepmother's will that accounted for all this; I suppose both factors were responsible. That's how it happened this time, too. When I entered the room where the children were still playing, Milkot was pacing the room, hands in his pockets.

"Here you are," he said, interrupting his pacing and stopping next to me. "Fancy meeting you here! Have you been forgiven already?"

"Yes," I said, swallowing my anger and suppressing the dislike I always experienced when I saw him. "Papa has forgiven me."

"If you were mine, I'd have dealt with you differently," he said, resuming his pacing.

"I'm not yours," I shot back at him.

I went up to the children and wanted to sit down and take part in their game, without regard to the fact that I didn't enjoy their friendship and had an implacable enemy in the person of Katya, the

Velins' eldest daughter. She couldn't stand me because, of all the children, I alone never submitted to her will, didn't fetch her toys on command, didn't pick up her handkerchief – in a word, I didn't behave like her servant. She was a genuine future mistress and, in spite of the fact that she was only ten years old, she deeply despised me, the daughter of her governess. Her parents' spoiled child, she snapped endless orders to her brothers and sisters and carried considerable weight in the household. The maids fulfilled her every whim, fearing her complaints. She didn't often obey my stepmother, who was frequently forced to yield to her in order to keep her parents' affection and not quarrel with them. Encountering in me alone opposition to her unlimited exercise of power, and being incapable of conquering me like all the others, she was unable to forgive my unwillingness to yield and my childish self-reliance and independence; therefore, she turned all the children under her charge against me. Often, after quarreling with me, she would forbid her brothers and sisters to play with me, shower me with sarcastic remarks after I was released from my punishments, and, at every possible opportunity, express her contempt for me, calling me a wicked, stubborn, poor child allowed to study with them only out of the goodness and charity of her mother's heart. "What are you?" she would often ask me. "Your mother is a governess – you have nothing at all – you live off other people's money, while we have our own! My father's rich! I'm rich – we pay you!" and ho 7.

I still didn't understand things very clearly and merely took offense at her insulting words. I never submitted to her and lived in open hostility with all the children. When I approached them and wanted to join them on the gathered chairs, Katya shouted to me:

"If you want to play with us, sit back there – the front seats are all taken."

"There's a place next to you," I said.

"I'm telling you to sit back there; there's no place for you here. Be content with the fact that we still let you play with us. Everyone knows you're a good-for-nothing."

"What sort of a good-for-nothing am I?" I asked heatedly, still annoyed by my recent punishment.

"Not only are you a person of no account, you get punished every day and locked in closets. They beat you and whip you, but it doesn't make you any better. Respectable children shouldn't play with ones who get beaten."

"If they could ever punish you, you'd be punished all the time," I said. "You get into more mischief than I do. Who broke a vase yesterday? Not me! Who hit Varya? Not me! Who didn't know her lesson this morning and said stupid things to the teacher? Not me! It was you!"

"Weakling! She's just a weakling! Just look at her, she's so angry! Ooh, ooh, ooh! You snake!" cried Katya, pointing her finger at me.

All the children took up the cry: "Ooh, ooh, ooh!" and pointed their fingers at me. I was beside myself with rage, my hands trembled, and I threw myself at Katya and tried to drag her off her chair. She shoved me away forcefully – she was two years older, a big girl, and strong for her age – I fell down and hit my head painfully on a chair, but scrambled to my feet at once and threw myself at her with frantic zeal. She let out a loud yell and, still fighting with me, began to cry. Milkot, pacing the floor all this while and not interfering in our affairs, even though he must have seen and heard everything, grabbed me and held me tight; flushed from the effort, I struggled desperately in silence in his arms. He carried me to my stepmother's room and coldly stood me on the floor; I wanted to escape into the drawing room again, but he held onto my arm and said to my stepmother:

"Take her away, Madame Stein. The children were fighting with her again – they were playing very nicely until she came in; then a new squabble broke out. If this reaches Madame Velina, she'll be most displeased. I'll try to soothe Katya: she's very upset. She's crying and wants to complain to her mother."

"Please, try to calm her down," my stepmother said to him. "Thank you, my friend," she added.

My father was no longer in the room. My stepmother was very angry; as soon as Milkot left, she grabbed my arm, squeezed it tightly, took me upstairs to the nanny's room, and punished me severely.

The next morning at tea Natalya Andreevna Velina said to my mother:

"Madame Stein, your Antonina has an awful disposition. She's always fighting with my children – make her stop, I beg you. It's all the more curious, since my children are usually so gentle, especially Katya."

"I already punished my daughter yesterday," said my stepmother. "I assure you that I'll be even stricter with her in the future and won't allow her to play with your children if she doesn't behave better. Antonina," she said, turning to me, "beg Mademoiselle Catherine's pardon immediately."

I turned pale and remained silent, not stirring from my place.

"Do you hear what I'm saying to you?" my stepmother continued menacingly. "Or was yesterday's punishment not sufficient?"

I didn't budge and sat there in silence. Papa, who was drinking tea at the same table, intervened and ordered me to ask Katya's forgiveness at once. I glanced up at him and, meeting his gaze, stood up immediately; my stepmother took me by the arm and led me over to Katya, who was sitting quietly and proudly on her own special, tall chair and could therefore look down at me. She was triumphant: I could read that in the proud gaze she fixed on me.

"Well, ask her forgiveness," my stepmother said to me, squeezing my arm in a way so expressive that even I understood.

"Forgive me," I said in a trembling voice, and a flood of tears drowned my words – they were bitter tears for a person of any age, tears of impotence and rage.

"Gladly," said Katya readily. Bending over, she extended her cheek for a kiss of reconciliation.

I backed away, as if she'd wounded me.

"You refuse?" she asked. "As you wish. I've done my duty."

"You're such a sweet child," my stepmother said to her. "She doesn't deserve your affection. She's wicked and stubborn. But I don't indulge her vices. Go to your room," she said, turning to me, "and don't leave it until I say so." *bitch*

"Come here, Katya," said Madame Velina. "Always be nice, my child, and always forgive insults – God will bless you for that."

I overheard these words as I was leaving the room – and from that time I ceased to value and understand people's sense of fairness, their impartial judgment, and their opinions. Thus passed my childhood; such scenes were repeated very frequently, but they didn't destroy my character – on the contrary, I developed inflexibility and was constantly racked by feelings of hatred, rage, and disgust mixed with fear. My father's caresses gradually lost their power over me and ceased softening my disposition; it seemed that with each passing day he withdrew further from me. I don't know if it was his illness or the endless struggle that killed him – probably both. He soon left for Moscow to undergo treatment, as it was explained in the house. He said farewell to me one evening: I vaguely remember waking up at night and seeing his sad, sickly face bent over my little bed. I can't say for sure whether it was a dream or reality. But when I got up the next morning, I couldn't find him – his room was empty, a few papers were scattered about the floor with some litter. I wept and, when I asked about him, was told he was gone. For a few months after his departure I lived more peacefully; they seemed to have forgotten all about me, and I got some relief. My stepmother was busy with Madame Velina's children, conducted lessons in music and French, and spent all her free time with Milkot, chatting or pacing the drawing room with him when the children were playing, or strolling in the garden with him. But don't think I was doing well – it's true I wasn't being punished as much as before, not beaten as often. I was able to rest physically, but I suffered a great deal of moral oppression. So many affronts, unjust reproaches, insults of all kinds! Do you know what it's like to be the daughter of a governess? It's like being everyone's Cinderella or, worse, a pariah; even if a small portion of mother's love were to lighten the load, her fate would still be far from enviable. This unfortunate creature is destined to serve everyone, from the mistress of the house to the lowliest maid; she's obliged to please everyone, endure everything, and feel sincerely and profoundly grateful for every crumb, because she has no right to anything. She's merely tolerated in the family, merely tolerated in a household where even the servants vent on her their dissatisfaction with the masters or her parents; endless persecution is the lot of such a child; whatever happens among the children of the family – a communal prank, intentional disobedience – she's always to blame. She's seen as the instigator and punished as an example to the rest; she *souffre douleur* [endures torments] from both young and old, is subordinate to everyone, and is always at the disposal of all the children. And do you know what children are like? They are the most pitiless, terrible, instinctual torturers, inflexible in principle because obstinacy governs them uncontrollably; once allowed, it becomes their law for a very long time, until the age when reason takes over and replaces their original obtuse, irrational stubbornness. But reason arrives late; until then, what doesn't a creature suffer at their hands? – a creature delivered to them as a victim, one they're used to considering as inferior, and one who's given over to their pleasure. You can easily imagine what I had to bear in that life with a character such as mine – the sufferings I endured. From early childhood I learned painfully to recognize all the various levels of society, crossing them with effort and overcoming them. Mine was the last place at the table; the most worthless crumbs fell to me. If treats were distributed to the children, they gave me one after everyone else, as if I were getting the leftovers, like a lapdog. But my lot was even worse – a dog is caressed, but I wasn't. Sometimes I categorically refused such humiliating handouts with wicked pride that was often interpreted as envy or rudeness. If we went for a walk, I felt ashamed at being so poorly dressed and lagged behind. If we went for a ride, I was always assigned the worst possible place. But I never got used to this endless series of humiliations among those proud, spoiled children. I endured it all with cold-blooded indignation and never grew fond of the people around me; I came to hate many of them. No one worried about me, caressed me, or consoled me in my childish, though still brutal, misfortunes. All the energy of my young life was concentrated on my father. I thought about him frequently, never heard anyone mention his name, and, because of a strange but powerful feeling, I never inquired about him, as if by doing so I feared defiling my love for him. About six months after his departure my stepmother received a letter from him – he asked her insistently to send me to him in Moscow. She prepared for the journey and accompanied me. I remember the terrible change we encountered – he was a mere shadow of his former self; coming out to meet us, he could hardly climb back upstairs: his breathing was labored and he was extremely weak. He lived in the apartment of a French family whom he had known for a long time. Madame Beillant was then a young widow, the eldest daughter in the household; she was particularly attached to my father, looked after him, read him books in the evening, and amused him as best she could. We lived there with them – my father occupied three small rooms separated from the main quarters by a cold landing. In the evening my stepmother would often visit old friends and acquaintances, while my father stayed at home with me and Madame Beillant and seemed much calmer. We spent two months there with him; I didn't notice any major changes – he was just very weak and didn't get out of the large armchair from which he was carried to bed at night, but I heard it said that he was getting worse. One evening after my step-mother left the room for a minute, he called me over and said:

"Ninochka, do you know what I'm thinking – what I've been thinking for some time?"

"No, Papa, I don't," I said.

"I want to go far away, Ninochka. Do you want to come with me back to my own country?"

"I do, Papa," I said with indescribable joy and fell at his knees.

"You don't know, you can't even imagine how nice it is there. You probably don't remember Mainz – you were so little when we brought you here. There are no endless snows, no heavy, leaden air, so wearisome – it's hard to breathe here, my dear. There, the Rhine flows through fertile valleys; even the sky is better."

His voice broke off from exertion and tenderness – tears welled up in his dimming eyes.

"Yes, yes," he continued quietly. "We'll go there – I feel better; a little while ago I thought I was dying, but this was merely a sick man's dream. I've decided to arrange everything tomorrow – and we'll leave. Today I'll talk with my wife about it."

"She won't let me go," I said, bursting into tears.

"No, I'll take you away. We'll leave together."

My stepmother came into the room with Madame Beillant and offered him some tea.

He didn't reply; instead he began talking insistently about his intention to leave as soon as possible and to take me with him. To my great surprise, my stepmother didn't raise the slightest objection and immediately agreed to everything. I was merely struck by her gloomy, uncharacteristic appearance and the dejection with which she looked at him. Madame Beillant just stood there, suppressing sobs with her handkerchief, and then hurriedly left the room. My father wanted to lie down; he caressed me tenderly as he said good-bye. His final words were memorable:

"Farewell, Nina," he said. "God be with you. Tomorrow, when you open your eyes, remember that a new life is about to begin for us – a peaceful one under the clear sky of my sweet native land. Yes, Ninochka, we'll leave for Mainz and we'll be very happy there!"

The next day, when I opened my eyes, a profound silence prevailed in the room – my stepmother wasn't to be found; when I looked around, I saw that her bed was still made, as if she hadn't slept in it. Our maid came in; her eyes were red from crying; she quickly helped me to dress, threw a coat around me, and without answering any of my questions, took me to the other side of the house. There people were walking around incessantly, whispering, quietly conversing; in spite of my agitated curiosity, I couldn't make out what they were saying. Madame Beillant saw me, took me onto her lap, and wept bitterly; my stepmother came into the room soon afterward and was also crying. I looked around wildly at all the sad faces, but didn't dare ask any questions. The impression of tormenting fear I felt so early and forcefully, of foreboding deep within my heart threatening something unknown and terrible, struck me so powerfully at the time that for the rest of my life I've acquired the habit of taking fright as soon as I see sad faces and downcast expressions. I don't rush to ask what it all means. First I try to read on the faces of those present the fate that menaces me; only then do I advance to meet it, after arming myself with fortitude and strength, and inquire as to what has happened with the courage of despair. But at that time I sat in the corner; seeing that my stepmother was talking quietly with one of her acquaintances, I began listening in on their conversation.

"Yesterday he was planning to leave for Mainz," said my stepmother. "Lately that was his favorite idea, his only one."

"Yes, yes," replied my stepmother's acquaintance. "Several hours before death consumptives always think they're completely cured – it's the first sign that the end is near. Well, did he suffer a great deal?"

"Oh, no. He fell asleep peacefully and didn't wake up," said my stepmother.

"Mama," I cried out suddenly in a piercing voice, rushing over to her from my corner. "Mamenka, where's Papa? I want to see him."

Madame Beillant came up to my stepmother and said something I didn't understand or couldn't hear. Seeing that no one answered my cry, I rushed to the door. I was forcibly restrained. My stepmother sat me down on her lap and began comforting and consoling me; meanwhile, Madame Beillant knelt in front of me and, sobbing, kissed me and said that my father had passed away during the night. I still didn't understand, having no real understanding of death. It was explained to me as it usually is to children. My despair at hearing this news was so powerful that I fell ill and delayed my stepmother's departure from Moscow. When my health was no longer at risk and I'd gradually begun to recuperate, she left immediately, entrusting me to Madame Beillant, who was extremely kind and loved me very dearly. My recovery proceeded slowly and she made every effort on my behalf; I spent some of the best days of my life in that kind family, where so many people took such good care of me. A few months later my stepmother returned to Moscow but didn't live with us; she came to visit me every day and was very affectionate. Once she had a long talk with Madame Beillant, after which both of them comforted me more than usual, and Madame Beillant had tears in her eyes. The next day my stepmother came to see us again wearing a splendid dress, no longer in mourning, and told me that in a week she'd take me home and soon we'd be going to live in the country. All the following week I saw her only once and then only for a minute; one morning, two or three days after that visit, Madame Beillant had me put on a white dress and took me to see my stepmother. Along the way she said some mysterious things, most of which I didn't understand, and several times she repeated:

"Be careful, Antonina, not to cry; don't upset your mama. She shouldn't have to tell you to obey and be quiet. Everything is as God wills it."

She got out of the carriage and, taking me by the hand, led me to my stepmother; we stayed there less than half an hour. Then, bidding me a tearful farewell, she made the sign of the cross over me, had me promise to be alert and obedient, to write her often; then she left. My stepmother lived in two rooms, reasonably well furnished, but there were signs that a departure was imminent. Suitcases stood in the corners of the room, dresses were spread out on tables and chairs, and I was particularly surprised to see some men's clothes and other items among them. I imagined that these were Papa's things and asked my stepmother about them, scarcely able to restrain my tears.

"Yes," she told me, "these things belong to your new father."

"What?" I asked, not understanding a thing.

"You're a sensible girl," she said. "Madame Beillant told me that you've become very smart, poised, and obedient. Show me that and I'll come to love you. You see, you're still little and don't understand very much; you must rely on me for everything and trust me. Just as it was impossible for you to continue living as an orphan, I, too, had to choose a new protector and friend. Well, I've chosen a worthy man and now he's become your new papa."

"I don't want him," I said, still not understanding very clearly. "I don't need him, Mama, I don't," I repeated, regarding my stepmother, no doubt with distress, because she took me onto her lap and said with greater tenderness:

"Ninochka, it can't be changed; he'll be a father to you and you'll come to love him – promise me that!"

I still didn't understand and began crying.

"Why are you crying?" my stepmother asked in a different tone of voice.

Just at this moment the door opened and in walked Milkot. He was wearing a tailcoat, a white tie, and a black vest. His outfit startled me – he appeared even more severe and terrifying. Coming up to my stepmother, he squeezed her hand and said:

"Well then?"

"Antonina," my stepmother said emphatically, letting me down from her lap and handing me over to Milkot, who took me in his arms. "Here's your new papa; give him a kiss." FUCK NO

How can I express what I experienced at that moment? I felt dread and bitterness; I was filled with indescribable horror mixed with disgust and anger. I began struggling in Milkot's arms, like the time he took me to my stepmother after the quarrel with Katya. At this recollection, entering my mind all of a sudden and for no apparent reason, my contempt for him increased. He tried to kiss me, but I bent my body, threw back my head, and cried out dreadfully, still trying to free myself from his embrace. He fixed his gaze on me, calmly lowered me to the floor, and left the room without saying a single word; my stepmother followed him. I remained alone and sat there until dinner, continuing to weep incessantly. At long last someone opened the door and said that Mrs. Milkot was waiting for me; I shuddered at the sound of this new name, realizing that it referred to my stepmother. I went into the drawing room and found them both seated at the table.

"Come here," Milkot said to me in his shrill voice. "I forgive your first reaction; now your duty is unquestioning obedience and respect for me and your mother. If you don't fulfill this obligation – things will get worse for you. You know I don't like pranks; now sit down and eat."

I sat down but couldn't eat a thing. I felt dazed and afraid of Milkot, having finally understood that now I was in his hands, entrusted to him entirely. When his cold, large, passionless eyes came to rest on me, I felt the same agitation, as well an irresistible desire to glance up at him timidly, the same feelings, it's said, a bird has when a snake, condemning it to a sacrificial death, drags it with incomprehensible strength into its greedy open jaws.

We left a few days later and settled down once again in the same region, in the same house. They didn't pay much attention to me during the first few months of their marriage; I noticed that my stepmother submitted to Milkot's influence completely; his will became her law – she did nothing without his permission. He gave English and German lessons to Madame Velina's children. Soon he announced that it was time for me to begin my own studies. I was then nine years old; this was a terrible period in my life and I shall attempt to recount it for you here in a few words. You already know how I feared and hated Milkot; my relations with him were extremely cold and barely civil. I never kissed him; when I would enter the classroom in the morning, I'd curtsy to him timidly, then sit down to my lessons immediately without saying a word. He was very demanding; if I didn't understand something, he explained it very patiently, but if my memory failed or I made a mistake in even one word, he was implacable.

"Do you understand?" he would ask after expounding on something.

"I do," I replied.

"Then learn it so that in an hour (sometimes he said two, depending on the amount and difficulty of the material) it will be all ready."

Later, after the time had passed, he asked me just as coldly and serenely:

"Have you learned it all?"

If I hadn't managed to do so, he sometimes gave me a reprieve of half an hour, which, however, was totally useless, because I couldn't learn anything when I felt so tormented by fear and anxiety. If I answered his question in the affirmative, he would listen to me recite. At the first mistake he would look at me with his terrible, cold eyes that caused me so much trepidation; my thoughts became muddled, my memory refused to serve me, and very often I would make another mistake.

"Be careful!" he would say.

Then fear would overcome me completely. In spite of all my efforts, I would inevitably make another mistake. He would immediately turn his head toward the door, and his impassive, metallic voice would ring out:

"Madame Milkot! Madame Milkot!" he cried. My stepmother came in.

"We've earned a reward today," he said calmly.

My stepmother took my hand and, without saying a word, led me upstairs; there she locked me in my room for the whole day and, instead of dinner, I was given bread and water. Sometimes there were variations in the punishments – they made me kneel in a corner of the room where the children were playing during recess, so that shame would be added to the physical pain. If Milkot pronounced the word "reward" with special emphasis, or even "exemplary reward," I was sure to be beaten with birch rods. I never asked for mercy and I cried only from pain; soon after the punishment I became completely calm. I entered a state of total insensibility, as happens when someone experiences an unavoidable misfortune, but one known well in advance. The rest of the day I was in no danger. After dinner I was given an enormous addition to do; if I made the slightest mistake, Milkot, who corrected it, would erase the entire sum. Handing me the slate, he would say calmly, "Do it again." I would have to rack my brains over these calculations, depending on how successful I was. In the evening for the most part I would fall fast asleep, worn out, suffering from a bad headache. The children's jokes and ridicule no longer affected or disturbed me as before; my character became calmer and my outbursts were no longer accompanied by tears or any other outward manifestations; everything was buried deep within me. I almost always sat alone; I became unsociable and morose, and never played or frolicked in the company of the other children. In the summer I would walk in the garden and, wandering alone or sitting by the meadow, would ask myself if this was the way all children of governesses had to live. A comparison between me and Madame Velina's family was almost impossible; I saw that they lived amid affluence, love, parental affection, and permissive tutors. I had to consider myself excluded from this privileged class. I remember that several times my stepmother said something to Milkot in my defense, probably taking pity on my bitter lot; but in those rare instances, he looked at her coldly and repeated his words distinctly, as if making her realize how inappropriate all her objections were. She never dared voice another protest and obeyed his will blindly. She had always been capricious and willful with my late father, but Milkot broke her will with his inflexible, cold, cruel rule and imperceptibly reduced her to complete obedience. She loved and feared him – probably her nature was one that required severity because she submitted to him with love. Regarding his behavior toward me, I'm sure he insisted on punishing me constantly on principle, sharing in this case the convictions of many people, especially the English, who are firmly convinced that it's impossible to raise children without beatings, birch rods, and other such punishments. In addition, he couldn't stand me; as a result, no feeling of pity ever entered his heart or mitigated his strict rules; for four years he punished me mercilessly.

When I turned thirteen, he stopped giving me lessons. I continued studying music and literature with my stepmother and, after these lessons, would return to my own room. I had a small, rectangular room with one window; my bed stood along the wall next to a table and a little chair. There was a large library in the house; I was told to occupy my time reading the classics, the choice to be made by Milkot. But I managed to obtain other books as well. I read all day, copied out passages, wrote summaries, and, after exhausting myself with this work, sat on my small chair and reflected – most often about my father, a pale, poetic figure whom I could imagine so vividly that I seemed to see him before me. His melancholy face and wonderful eyes never left me and seemed to follow me everywhere; I asked my stepmother for his portrait, hung it on the wall opposite the table where I worked, and used to gaze at it for a long time, a very long time. My heart, thirsting so eagerly for attachment and love, found nourishment in these memories of my deceased father. I loved him more and more: of course, it was all just a dream, but it sweetened and supported my existence. Solitude, reading, and music filled my life and turned me into a mature adult well before my time. Often at twilight I went into the empty parlor, sat down to play the piano, and listened to the music; my soul would yearn to fly somewhere far away and I'd suffer twice as much, but all the same, I took pleasure in that suffering.

Relations with my stepmother were cold; she frequently reproached me for every trifle, scolded me for the least neglect of Milkot's wishes, sparing neither words nor phrases, while, at the same time, Milkot's behavior toward me gradually and imperceptibly began to change. As soon as I stopped taking lessons, he no longer supported my stepmother's decrees. When she scolded me – he would remain an indifferent spectator, never interfering in our disagreements. Later, when I turned fifteen, he began to intervene mildly on my behalf. It finally reached the point when something resembling an affectionate word would escape his lips; he noticed that I'd become meek and sensible, as well as very pretty. As a child I was pale and jaundiced, skinny and short; but at the age of fifteen I suddenly began getting taller, filling out, taking shape, and my complexion became translucent and bright. Our guests, neighboring landowners, were surprised at the sudden change and offered me many compliments. At first, neither I nor my stepmother noticed the modification in Milkot's attitude; but when his solicitude grew, it became burdensome to me and unpleasant to my stepmother; consequently, she began to treat me even more coldly and severely. Twice between her husband and her something resembling a quarrel occurred; with unaccustomed firmness she said that he shouldn't interfere in her relations with me. On another occasion she grew even more angry and, with great passion that reminded me of her married life with my late father, she declared that in order to avoid any arguments in the future, she was planning to send me away. I took advantage of this opportunity: the next day, finding her alone, I asked if I could seek a position as a governess in another household. My stepmother agreed immediately and began to search for an opening. A neighboring landowner was seeking a governess for his elder children: he was Velin's cousin and lived fifty versts* away. My stepmother was very glad of the opportunity and reached an agreement with him immediately. I don't know why, but she seemed to make all the arrangements in secret from her husband. By mutual agreement, unspoken and merely conjectured, neither I nor my stepmother ever mentioned it in Milkot's presence. But he soon found out; one morning he came into my room.

"Antonina," he said, "why do you want to leave us? I've spoken with your mother and told her you're too young to live with someone else. But she maintains it's something you want to do and not her idea."

"Yes," I replied, "I do wish to live alone, all by myself. I'm almost seventeen – I can earn enough money to support myself."

"Don't you like living with us? I don't mind paying your expenses and I do love you. As a child you were punished, but that's an inevitable evil, the fate of all children. It's impossible to raise anyone without strictness, especially a child who's fated to live in other people's homes. That child must learn to get used to everything very quickly; later on he will have to endure a great deal and will always depend on others. Don't you understand that I did all this for your own good?"

"Well, then," I said without replying to his last question, "you fulfilled your obligation in good conscience and now I'm ready to live with other people. After the education you've provided me, any kind of life, no matter how terrible, won't be hard to endure."

"Can't you use simpler terms?" he objected. "Even now, in reply to my concern, you repay me with irony."

"That which man sows, so shall he reap," I said coldly.

"Listen," he said, sitting down next to me and taking my hand against my will. "Let's talk without bitterness, if possible. Don't you see that since you've become a mature young woman, I'm prepared to become your friend and I always intervene on your behalf? Stay here with us: I promise your stepmother will be nicer to you."

"Thank you kindly for your sympathy," I replied, interrupting him and freeing my hand.

"Isn't it true that for some time now I've been trying to provide you with all manner of satisfaction, and, when your mother fails to restrain herself, I keep her in check?"

"Your efforts have been in vain," I replied. "I don't need your defense."

"I will be strict with her," he said again. "I'll force her to love you and cherish you as much as you deserve. Stay here with us."

"In other words, after persecuting me in my childhood, you're now prepared to tyrannize my stepmother. Aren't you tired of being the oppressor?" I protested in indignation. "Aren't you bored by the role?"

"You don't want to understand me. I want you to know that I love you like a daughter, a friend, and I came to . . . "

I smiled ironically. His expression changed and his eyes blazed.

"Let's end this unpleasant conversation," I said. "We aren't getting anywhere."

"Antonina!" he said, standing up. "You'll regret the fact that you've rejected my protection. Go and see what it's like to live in someone else's house, if that's what you want. You'll find out how difficult it is; I could prevent you from leaving, but I won't oppose your desire: later on I hope you'll be convinced that you were better off with us. Besides, who knows, perhaps you'll come back . . . "

"I'll try not to," I said.

He started walking slowly out of my room and met his wife at the door. She gave him a look of surprise mixed with restrained annoyance. She didn't say a word to him, but, turning to me, said curtly:

"They're sending their horses to fetch you in three days; pack your things – everything should be ready by then."

She turned and walked out. I understood clearly that my situation had become even more difficult.

Forgive me if I don't include all the details and hasten through this part of my life. It's painful to talk about, although even the least important circumstances are etched indelibly in my memory; but since these recollections are so hateful and oppressive, I will skip ahead. There's still a great deal to tell – much that is sad and distressing, and I must conserve my energy.

After this scene, so insignificant in words, yet so meaningful in expression, I spent my days never leaving my room, packing my things, appearing only at dinner. At long last, one inclement autumn day, I was informed that a carriage had come for me. All my belongings consisted of one small suitcase, a box with the portrait of my father, and a little sack. All this was quickly packed up and, as soon as the horses had been fed, I went to bid farewell to the master and mistress. I didn't love anyone in this house and left them all without regret. Then I set off to find my stepmother; she was having tea in her room, while Milkot was pacing.

"I've come to say good-bye to you," I said to her as I entered the room.

"Good-bye," she said. "I wish you happiness. You're beginning life on your own, all alone – remember that you must behave modestly and decently. You're free until you begin to act foolishly. If your behavior isn't satisfactory in all respects, I'll take you back and find you a place in a boarding school as a classroom teacher under strict control of a headmistress."

"I don't know," I said, "whether you have the right to do that. I have no parents; I'll live on my own earnings. Everyone has the right to live just as he chooses if he works for his own living."

"Antonina," my stepmother replied, "you've not been blessed by heaven. From your birth you've never loved anyone. You're leaving the house where you spent your whole childhood without tears or emotions that usually accompany such a departure. You're ungrateful and obstinate: try as I did, I was unable to change you. God grant you happiness, but God doesn't bless disobedient children – remember that."

Milkot paused opposite my mother and stared at her – she fell silent. I couldn't see his face: he was standing with his back toward me.

"Thank you," I said, "but you can't really predict the future. I'm superstitious. Let me leave without your predictions that sound more like maledictions to me." My voice faded away.

"My God! What a woman," cried my stepmother, folding her arms. "And she's only sixteen – what a black sheep!"

"Enough!" Milkot threatened her and then, coming up to me, added, "Good-bye, Antonina. I wish you happiness."

"Likewise," I replied coldly, bowed, and left the room.

No one escorted me except my maid: she alone, bidding me farewell, shed tears. I don't know whether she felt pity for me, or if habit dictated that she consider it her decided duty to cry at every departure.

The carriage crawled slowly through the mud, swaying from side to side. The coachman shouted to his nags; it was drizzling and the cold was biting. I had only a light cloak and a worn-out old hat, poor protection from the damp and wind. But I wasn't thinking about any of this – my thoughts were far away and my heart was filled with secret indignation and suppressed malice. I wasn't pleased with myself. What would my real father say if he'd witnessed such a farewell scene? Leaving my stepmother, I was unable to forgive her or be reconciled with the past; at long last I was free – why couldn't I forgive them for my childhood and my sad, oppressive youth? My score with them was settled – why couldn't I judge them more generously? True, my stepmother had never treated me like a daughter – but I wasn't really her daughter. So we were quits. Why did I leave her and that house with such deep rancor? Those were the thoughts that tormented me on my journey.

We arrived late and found the gate locked. The coachman climbed down from his box and began knocking with impatient insistence. At last the yardman's grumbling could be heard and he came to open the gate. The carriage entered the courtyard and stopped near the entrance. I got out. The door was locked, so the knocking began again. The door was opened for us, too. We were greeted by a sleepy man in a greatcoat.

"Who's this?" he asked the coachman. "Have you brought the mam'selle?"

"Obviously," replied the coachman. "Why did you lock the gate? Didn't you know enough to expect us? We really had to bang."

"Why in hell did you come after midnight? All the good folk are sound asleep. They couldn't sit up waiting for you all night," growled the man. "As if a mam'selle's all that important!"

》 《

"You smile," Antonina said, looking at Ilmenev. "And you, my friend, look at me in such an intense, sad way," she added, glancing tenderly at the deep sympathy reflected in Pletneev's face. "But none of this affected me at the time. From childhood I'd grown used to the masters' pride, the servants' rudeness, insolent demands from the masters' children, family oppression, beatings – what else is there? I got used to everything, my friends! Consequently, these words didn't upset me, nor did this reception surprise me. One house is just like another. It's the same everywhere – the faces change but the substance remains the same."

》 《

I entered the hallway and felt only terrible exhaustion and a strong chill.

"Where's my room?" I asked the man who'd opened the door and greeted me so cordially.

"Just wait a minute," he said sternly. "First I'll lug your things in, then go rouse the housekeeper."

I sat on a bench. The hallway was dirty; a bucket filled with slops had probably acquired rights of citizenship some time ago, since a constant puddle and spots on the floor around it bore witness to the fact that it had stood in that same place forever. The man dragged in my suitcase and box.

"Is this all?" he asked.

"Yes."

"Well, let's go upstairs."

He led me along a corridor, walking carefully, and cautioning, "Don't wake the master and mistress." I followed him up a steep staircase and found myself in front of a locked door. He left and went back downstairs; I felt extremely tired and sat down on the top step. He took an age; he finally returned with the key and unlocked the door.

"Fyokla says everything's ready and there's no need for her to come," he said to me.

I went in. There actually was a large quilt on the bed, as well as some pillows, but there were no linens on them. With the help of my guide I untied the knots of the cords fastening my suitcase, and then, after spreading a sheet over the quilt, sent the man away, locked the door, undressed quickly, and jumped into bed. I fell into the deep slumber known only to weary youth, no matter how unhappy they may be. When I opened my eyes, it was already light and the pale rays of the autumn sun filled my room, flooding it freely in the absence of drapes. I didn't know the time, so I hurried to get dressed and go downstairs, where I found the entire Chernetsov family gathered in the parlor at a round table having their morning tea. I'd known them for a long time; they were related to the Velins and had often come to visit us. The family consisted of an elderly mistress, Glafira Vasilevna, her husband, Ivan Sidorovich, and their four children: one son and three daughters, my future pupils.

"Here you are, my dear," the mistress said affectionately. "Welcome! What luck! Sit down and have some tea."

She poured a cup and handed it to me and asked about the journey. She apologized for our having had to knock so long at the gate last night, adding that the roads were in bad condition, very bad this autumn, that it had been drizzling constantly, so how could they possibly be in good condition? Her husband shared this opinion and concluded that the neighboring peasants were all knaves and didn't keep the bridges in good repair. Then we all fell silent and drank tea in imperturbable serenity.

"Well, now," Glafira Vasilevna said, getting up from the table, "I shall introduce my children to you. Varinka, Sashur, come here: this is Antonina Mikhailovna. Say hello to her; come to love and obey her. And you, too, my dear, be kind to them. They're good children and obedient; you'll be pleased with them. Take a few days to get to know them and then you can begin your lessons. You won't have to worry about the two youngest: each has her own nanny. I ask you only one thing – never leave them alone, be with them all the time, and speak French to them."

It was difficult for me to get used to the idea of being a governess. I had no trouble giving lessons. I was patient and gentle, but the children's games, the need to follow them constantly from room to room, their strolls and outings in good weather – all that was unbearable; and these activities were part of my responsibilities. At nine o'clock in the evening the children went to bed, and I retired to my own room, where I could finally occupy myself, but not for long. The children got up early and I had to be present at their dressing and morning prayers. Still, I considered myself fortunate because I was left alone: no one's gaze burdened me, no one's reproaches upset me, no one's interference made me anxious. Glafira Vasilevna, seeing my perpetual gentleness with the children, my constant modesty in the circle of her acquaintances, and my submissiveness to her will in everything concerning the children, grew attached to me and began to treat me as if I were a member of the family. She was not a very intelligent woman, but a very good one; as far as her husband was concerned, I saw him only at dinner and at evening tea, after which he disappeared. Rumors circulated in the house that he liked to nap after dinner and that he was an excellent master at all other times of the day.

In this monotonous way my life passed, but I had no intention of complaining. I rejoiced at being so far from my stepmother and her husband; when I did see them, I took care to avoid further explanations with him and arguments with her. We visited the Velins fairly frequently and spent whole weeks as their guests; sometimes they came to see us, but since I had a specific place in the Chernetsov household, I exercised my independence with great enjoyment. My stepmother, seeing me so well loved and respected, changed her attitude toward me and became more affectionate, but Milkot became even stranger. It's hard for me to describe his behavior; there was no intimacy between us and never could be. Having spent seven years together in my childhood, we never once exchanged even a few kind words. His voice aroused a shudder in me: I always heard in its dry, metallic tone something resembling the blows that showered down on me so generously when he pronounced his first verdict. The executioner of my childhood, he was now trying to become the patron of my adamant, somewhat contemptuous coldness. In the presence of strangers and my stepmother, he was only amicably polite; but as soon as he found me alone, he became very tender, paid me compliments, and flattered my vanity. I avoided him as best I could. I'm convinced that if I could have been a little more affectionate, he'd have been able to save me from a great deal later – but how can one be sure of that?

Two years passed while I lived at the Chernetsovs; it was Christmas and we set off to visit the Velins. We were supposed to remain there until the New Year. One morning Milkot came into my room, handed me a parcel, and said:

"Antonina, you love nice clothes; there's soon to be a ball in our neighborhood. I thought about you and ordered you some material for a fashionable new dress. Please accept my gift."

"Thank you," I said, rejecting the material wrapped in paper. "I don't need any dresses."

I don't know whether I've already told you that I loved fine clothes with the passion of a young child and the eagerness of a schoolgirl, and that this taste grew stronger inasmuch as I rarely had the opportunity to satisfy it. When I began receiving a salary, I had a number of dresses made and wore them with the pleasure young girls experience when they get dressed up for the first time and the enjoyment experienced by a person whose labor has allowed him to indulge both taste and desire. In spite of this recent increase in my wardrobe, I wasn't thinking about attending balls and didn't own a single ball dress.

"But I ordered this *barège** especially for you," he said, pursing his lips, which was the only visible sign of his aroused anger.

"Perhaps you did," I replied. "But since you did it without my consent, I can't be held accountable for the waste of money."

"It's not about money, but the insult. Yes, if you don't accept my gift, you'll be insulting me. Take it."

"I don't want it," I said decisively.

"Then I'll give it to your maid. She'll make herself a dress, put it on, and look like a decent young lady, while you'll look like a maid."

"I have enough dresses," I replied. "Even if I didn't, you'll recall that from childhood I was always dressed badly so I'm used to doing without. It's all so familiar to me," I added with cold pride.

He started to leave, but turned back at the door.

"Antonina," he said decisively. "I've been seeking your friendship for the last three years. Don't you want to make your peace with me? Let's be friends. Let's forget the past. Forgive me if I was to blame for anything."

"Never," I replied. "The past is still here, deep inside," I said, unintentionally pressing my hand to my heart.

"Antonina, consider: you're risking your life. Don't forget that I'm humbling myself and begging for your friendship. Be careful: I will never forgive you this humiliation."

I looked him straight in the eye.

"Really," I said with hatred. "Do you think your humiliation is something new? You've been humiliated since you chose to hate a child and became her immutable and implacable tormentor. You had me beaten – I despised you even then."

He turned extremely pale.

"Ah!" he said indistinctly. "You want hostility, struggle, unyielding hatred – fine; but you should know that I'm powerful and will force you to lay your insolent head at my feet. You'll come to beg my forgiveness, but it'll be too late. For the last few years you've been pushing me into an abyss of hatred that I'd hoped to leave far behind – you're very foolish! You'll regret it, but it'll be too late, I tell you."

"We'll see!" I replied, fixing my indignant and hostile gaze on him.

He stared at me, too. Our eyes met – it was as if we were gauging each other's strength. Neither of us lowered his gaze nor blinked his eyes. He walked out of the room very slowly. Since then we haven't exchanged a single word.

We returned home the day after this conversation. Glafira Vasilevna definitely wanted to attend the ball, to which the whole district had been invited, and she asked me to come along. With great care I made myself a prim and proper white muslin dress with a matching belt. I wanted to look no worse than the others; even though I couldn't look grand, I wanted to have fresh attire. Glafira Vasilevna introduced me to many young ladies whom I didn't know; in accordance with her wishes, people treated me in a polite and protective manner, then left me standing in a corner of the room. The young gentlemen didn't pay me any attention, hardly invited me to dance, hardly spoke to me – after all, who was I really? A governess! No more! I should be honored by the invitation to attend the event, as if I were a young lady of noble origin.

Katya Velina was the belle of the ball, splendidly, elegantly dressed; full of self-importance, she paraded around the room arm in arm with other young girls.

"Here you are!" she said, seeing me. "Bravo! You're all done up! But why are you in white – like a sylph* in a ballet?"

"What of it? She's a very poetic creature," I replied. "Thank you for the compliment."

"How are your charges? Are they well? Good pupils?" she asked deliberately.

"Very well," I replied simply and began chatting with another girl.

"Who's that young lady?" someone asked Katya.

"She's no lady," Katya replied.

"Why did you ask her about her children?"

Katya started laughing.

"What should I ask her about?" she said. "She's a governess!"*

"Is that all?" someone replied.

Everyone laughed; later I heard this story, which everyone found so amusing, repeated several times.

Soon the music began. I sat at one end of the hall and looked sadly at the couples dancing. I hadn't been asked to dance and asked myself why I'd come, carried away by the desire for diversion, as if I could find a place among these rich young people and take part in their exclusive enjoyments, restricted to the wealthy elite. I was roused from my sad reflections by the sound of a tender, melodious voice.

"Permit me to invite you to a turn of the waltz."

My heart began pounding at the sound of this voice. It reminded me of the remote, unfamiliar resonance of my dear, kind father's voice, still vital, perpetually pleasant, stored deep within my soul. I glanced up: before me stood a tall, graceful officer with light blue eyes and wavy blond hair. He repeated his invitation. I stood up and my trembling hand found itself in his.

Do you believe in the first impression of first love at first glance, the first magnetic confluence of a gaze, and the momentary fusion as two kindred souls recognize each other? You don't? Well I don't either; nevertheless, this is precisely what happened to us. Why? How? I don't know. How could I? His voice awakened a revered memory; the color of his eyes and wavy hair revived a distant image; it seemed that in him my father was sending himself to me again. Of course, I understood all this afterward; at the time I was merely embarrassed and couldn't make out a word he was saying. But the sound of his voice, rather than the meaning of his words, penetrated my young soul, its eager yearning for love, my orphaned heart that knew not how to surrender or whom to love. I don't remember what he said to me, or what I replied; I remember merely that the evening flew by like one blessed moment, like a dream, and that I found myself later that night in bed wondering what was wrong with me. Unable to answer my own question, I got up, sat in a chair, and pondered. "How like my father he is! How very like!" The idea of love was still far off; but you must know that all the loving strings of my heart were touched, recollections awakened, and my impressionable nature powerfully affected. I didn't know it yet, but in fact I was already deeply in love.

The next day there was a dinner and a sleigh ride. They asked Glafira Vasilevna to stay, and she gladly agreed. He sat next to me at dinner; when everyone went for a ride, he sat me in his sleigh and drove his own troika* admirably. That evening we had a long chat; I candidly confessed that I was partial to him because he reminded me of my late father, not only in his looks, voice, and hair, but even his name – he was called Michel. He listened attentively and, seeing my expression change as I talked about my father, took my hand, squeezed it, and said something very sweet and tender. I started crying and left the room. When we met the next day after this conversation, it was as if we'd been acquainted for some time and were already good friends. He asked where I lived; later, when he said good-bye, he promised to visit the Velins soon, where we planned to stay a while.

When we left I was in a daze. On the way Glafira Vasilevna asked if I'd had a good time. I began to express my heartfelt thanks and, unable to restrain myself, threw my arms around her neck and burst into tears. She took this outburst as a simple expression of youthful gratitude and was so touched by it that she said:

"Listen, Ninochka" – that's what she'd called me for some time – "I love you as if you were my own elder daughter. Besides, you're so kind to my children and work so hard in spite of your youth, that I want to provide you with every possible enjoyment. If there are to be any gatherings or festivities in our neighborhood, I'll invite you to come along to all of them. Two or three days without lessons won't mean a thing – why, soon it'll be Varinka's birthday. I will organize a children's party and we'll also invite some adults. Now we'll have five days or so visiting the Velins; then we'll return home and organize this little affair. Are you pleased with me, my dear?"

"You're so kind," I replied, kissing her. "I don't know how to express my love."

What shall I tell you? He soon arrived at the Velins and spent two days with us there, then came to call on us. In a few visits he had succeeded in pleasing everyone and was invited to return often. Sometimes he spent a whole week or more at a time with us. You know that people get acquainted faster and grow closer in the country than in town. He and I became friends from our first glance and our mutual love grew quickly. I won't tell you his last name – what for? Fate and his own will and character subsequently parted us. I'll simply refer to him as Michel, as I always called him during the time of our love, our brief period of happiness.

He lived in a wealthy home belonging to his father's sister; he didn't have a mother, but there were two grown sisters who lived in Moscow with their aunt and their father. When he was commissioned as an officer, he came to Moscow on his annual leave. His father wanted him to pay a visit to his old, solitary grandmother, who adored him and lived in the provinces not far from us. That explains how he ended up in our remote district. When I made his acquaintance he was twenty-two years old; his character was gentle, tender, and kind, just like his physiognomy. Most likely I'd have come to love him later, if I hadn't fallen in love with him at first, because, living among people as insensitive as the Velins, with the cruel and inexorable Milkot and my stern, unloving stepmother, the ideal image that had formed in my head was of a man endowed with tenderness, limitless kindness, and sincerity; all this could be found in Michel. There was a great deal of femininity in him, and I revered that trait – I didn't regard it as a fault in a man, merely as the ultimate expression of kindness and sensitivity. Early on I understood that intelligence without straightforward, genuine goodness is both useless and harmful. Finding Michel so generously endowed in this respect, I loved him tenderly and was rapturously astonished by his gentle heart. But everyone liked him; he somehow arranged things so that when he came to visit us, it was like a holiday for everyone. The children rushed out to hug him, Glafira Vasilevna greeted him affectionately, and Ivan Sidorovich exchanged loud kisses with him in public. He helped Glafira Vasilevna lay out the cards for a game of solitaire and held the wool while she unwound it, accompanied her husband to inspect the livestock and chatted with him about the harvest and the household, built houses of cards with the children and played blindman's buff with them, and took me for sleigh rides, and in the evenings we played pieces for four hands on the piano. Even our old housekeeper, a terrible grumbler, grew to like him. He always had a kind word or a good-natured joke for everyone; he was soon completely at home with us.

His relations with me were amicable; although we knew that we loved each other, we never said a word about it. Taking such pleasure in the present, we didn't think about the future at all. But this is the happiest feature of first love, and perhaps the source of the ecstasy, poetry, and mystery of its freshness. To live a wonderful life in the fleeting moment, to enjoy rapturously and carelessly the happiness of being together, desiring nothing, and sinking into reverie – what can be compared to a time like that? We were fortunate it happened to us so early: how miserable, pathetic, and insignificant is the person who has never experienced this miraculous dream even once in his life? Later, if we fall in love, we hasten to analyze, calculate, formulate, knowing from experience that most things do not last, and thus we ourselves destroy the nicest flowers on the tree of life and love. But at that time I was young and loved beyond all measure; all of a sudden the life of my soul blossomed magnificently. I didn't notice anything around me and thought only of him.

After Christmas the sleigh rides ended – he went to visit his grandmother; two monotonous weeks ensued – I waited in vain for him every day. Another week passed; one evening I was sitting alone in the parlor leafing through a history book with the children, explaining the pictures, when a sleigh bell sounded in the distance. My heart began pounding; I listened apprehensively and heard it in the village and then bursting forth as it entered our courtyard. The children were startled and, like a flock of happy birds, rose up and flew into the entry hall. I sat still, tormented by expectation, hope, and a fear of being disappointed.

"Who is it?" asked Glafira Vasilevna, lowering her work to her knees.

"I really don't know," I replied, barely able to breathe.

"What is it, Ninochka? Why are you always so indifferent? Please, dear, go find out who it is – you never make haste. Is that like a young woman?"

I didn't hear what else Glafira Vasilevna said. I was grateful for the opportunity and went into the entry hall.

Michel was taking off his military greatcoat, its beaver collar covered in hoarfrost. The children surrounded him: Sasha hung around his neck, Varya tugged him affectionately by the hand, and the two youngest had fastened onto his sword. After quickly kissing each of them, he freed himself and came toward me. His face, laughing a moment ago, was filled with joyful, tender emotion.

"Mademoiselle Stein," he said. "Greetings. Try as I did to hurry back to you, I couldn't leave my grandmother for three weeks. It's been so long since we've seen each other."

He kissed my hand.

"Twenty days," we both said simultaneously, standing in the middle of the hall holding hands.

"An age!" he said, slowly releasing my hand, then quickly moving into the parlor where the children had already trumpeted his arrival.

"Ah, Mikhail Arkadich, is it you? At last! I thought you'd forgotten us," said Glafira Vasilevna.

"No, not at all. Now I've come for several days, and I even have the intention of abducting you," he replied.

"How so?" everyone asked with curiosity.

Then he said that his grandmother was organizing a gathering of all her neighbors for Shrovetide;* there would be carriage rides and masquerades. She was eager to amuse him before his departure.

"Are you going somewhere?" asked Glafira Vasilevna.

I felt a deathly chill run down my spine; I sat still, as if I'd turned to stone. He glanced at me, stood up nervously, and announced abruptly:

"Yes, it's time, I must be home for Lent." But then he came over to my corner of the room and added quietly, "Don't believe it."

Meanwhile, Glafira Vasilevna continued to lament his departure and declared that in that case she would definitely visit his grandmother.

He proposed going together, taking all the children, and staying at his grandmother's house until Shrovetide, especially since it was only a week and a half away. At first, Glafira Vasilevna didn't agree;

but when the children, Michel, and even I clustered around her, she finally promised to persuade her husband to undertake that general migration. Michel's grandmother lived about a hundred versts away; it was agreed that Glafira Vasilevna would accompany the children in one closed sleigh, while Michel, the children's nanny, and I would travel in an open one. I never could stand a closed vehicle: they make me dizzy. And to this I owe the very best moments of my life.

When Ivan Sidorovich returned and our intentions were explained, he didn't receive the plan very well; but our entreaties were so insistent that he finally yielded to the universal desire and promised that, after he had taken care of some household matters, he would join us before the end of Shrovetide. On the third day after Michel's arrival, preparations and efforts began; everything in the house was turned upside down. There was constant running up and down stairs, and general cheerful confusion prevailed; the children were beside themselves with joy and their mother regarded them with a kindly smile. As for me, I still feel buoyant when I recall these events. At the time it was as if I'd suddenly discovered a youth I'd never known; I felt it keenly, became familiar with its rapture, and warm blood seethed in my veins. I rushed around more than the others, laughed, joked, and packed my things; the children ran after me, and Michel followed. In general everyone in the Chernetsov household liked me; and, even though the old nanny was annoyed at all the commotion, grumbling at everyone, she still carefully packed my dresses too, while complaining that we weren't helping at all, merely getting in the way.

》 《

"My friends," Antonina said suddenly after a moment of silence filled with recollection. "How happy I was then!"

She fell silent once more and a stream of tears ran down her pale face. Pletneev kissed one hand and Ilmenev squeezed the other sympathetically. Masha sat immobile under the painful impact of Antonina's story. She gradually tried to calm herself and resumed her tale:

I've had the strength, my friends, to narrate my oppressive childhood to you, to describe my terrible youth and its tragic catastrophes, my poor marriage and the hard life that followed; but no, I have neither the strength nor the resolution to fix my gaze on these happy days, so busy, so short, so ecstatic! That time is long gone: twelve years have passed since then. Even now, talking about those days, tears well up in my eyes, my indefatigable heart pounds rebelliously and still suffers, and my former, stormy passion bursts into my soul with these remembrances! Tedious, profound, burning recollections oppress me. I don't love him any longer: love for my first friend died and grew cold long since, but even now, when I start talking about him, it's as if I begin to love him all over again! The human heart feels deeply – its innermost depths are immeasurable, dark, and strange; and that which is lost in it often comes to the surface unexpectedly and fills the whole being with long-lost, lifeless feeling. Where did I stop? Oh, yes – the departure.

》 《

We left two days later. Nanny sat in one corner of the sleigh, I was in the middle, and Michel sat next to me on the other. How solicitously he helped me in, asked whether I was comfortable, lowered my veil, covered me with furs, and was mortally afraid lest I catch a chill. Never had anyone taken such good care of me; do you know what it's like to experience the ardent, sincere attentions of one's beloved for the first time, especially for someone who's never known the tenderness of a mother, the love of sisters and brothers, the sympathy of friends? I could hardly answer his constant questions: I was so deeply moved! After covering some thirty versts, we had to change horses; at the station Michel jumped down from the sleigh and demanded new ones at once.

"Are you freezing to death?" he asked me. "Come in here and get warm – they're taking so long to harness the horses."

I started to climb down and had just stepped out onto the frame of the sleigh when I felt unsteady; he took me in his arms and carried me into the cottage. I was so ashamed, but at the same time it felt so good! He sat me down on the stove-bench* and began to unfasten and remove my coat. The coachmen told us that Glafira Vasilevna had preceded us by half an hour and gone on ahead, after changing horses. Our old nanny went off to have dinner and left me alone with Michel, who sat down next to me.

"You're cold, so cold," he said, taking my icy hands in his. Bringing them up to his glowing face, he warmed them with his breath.

Little by little he pressed them to his lips and bent his head over my lap. Without looking up at me, he whispered, "I love you, how I love you, Antonina!" I remained silent; I couldn't speak. His words found such a powerful resonance in my soul that large tears began coursing down my cheeks. He glanced up at me and, seeing my tears, squeezed my hand tightly.

"Tell me that you love me," he said.

I remained silent. Feelings of joy, rapture, love, and shame were so strong that I couldn't speak; but, pressing my head to his shoulder, I wept quietly.

"Antonina, do you hear me? I love you," he said again. "And you?"

"I . . . I love you, too," I said, barely audibly, my voice breaking from emotion.

The door, which had been frozen shut, suddenly opened with a loud bang. "The horses are ready," our coachman announced and immediately withdrew. Michel took my kerchief and covered my head, then sat me down on a chair and began to help me on with my fur-lined shoes; after having put one on, he kissed my foot; I made an involuntary gesture of fear and shame and pulled my foot away. Resting on his knees before me, he let go of my other foot; looking up at me with his clear eyes, he asked me timidly and tenderly:

"Are you angry?"

I was silent; my face burned brightly; after helping me on with my fur coat and fastening the collar, he said quietly:

"If you only knew how much I love you, you wouldn't reproach me for my audacity and wouldn't deny me the joy of kissing your little foot."

"Did I say anything?" I replied, lowering my gaze.

"You were frightened – isn't that the same? You don't know what you mean to me, how precious you are."

I was already dressed and ready to go.

"Well," he continued, "I won't dare carry you out again, if you won't allow it."

I headed for the door in silence – I was so ashamed, but at the same time so happy.

He followed me, helped me into the sleigh, and climbed in next to me. It began to grow dark. The horses raced ahead along a smooth, level road; the night was frosty and beautiful – the moon soon rose and lit up the road and snowy fields; it cast its silver rays playfully and filled the fields with its gentle light. Everything was so splendid all around us – inside us as well! We were silent for a long time, filled with rapture and ecstasy; but gradually we began chatting. Michel said he was putting his hope in the future; of course, much grief and many obstacles lay before us, but we would endure the grief and overcome all obstacles. He was very sure of himself and was counting on me; his aunt loved him deeply and would of course agree with his decision, once convinced of our love.

"And your father?" I asked timidly.

"My father listens to my aunt on all matters; he's always at her house. She raised us and is very wealthy. My father's not very well-off and owes her everything. If she agrees, he will, too. My aunt loves me so much – how can she not yield to my entreaties? But you must be strong and patient."

"Oh, I'm yours; nothing will ever come between us," I said, "neither persecution nor reproaches; persecution isn't new to me and reproaches are an old story."

"My poor Ninochka," he said with a tear in his eye, "what haven't you experienced! Wait a little while longer – our time will come, it will!"

》 《

It has, my friends, but not as expected and not as he predicted; it wasn't he who was my defender, not he who was my savior!

》 《

"I'm afraid," he continued. "You're so quiet and meek. Are you up to the struggle?"

"Don't be afraid," I replied. "Don't worry about me; I can endure anything."

"My dear," he said again. "No, no, where are the words to express my love, my boundless love – they don't exist in human speech!"

Thus we passed that night, that wonderful night. Like real children we talked and wept to our hearts' content, especially I, so aware of my own happiness and bliss; at last we grew tired and fell peacefully asleep sitting next to each other. My head rested on his shoulder, his head, on my hat. We had already arrived at the gate of the house when they woke us up; on the horizon a bloodred sun was rising, casting its glow on our surroundings. Michel escorted me to the door of the room prepared for me – the proprietors were still fast asleep, but the servants were up and cleaning the house. He helped me to get settled, had my things carried up, and when all this was done, asked for some tea. His valet brought in a samovar;

we made tea and drank it slowly, wishing to postpone our parting, as if we wouldn't see each other the next day. We sat on the sofa in silence for a long time, filled with happiness; at last he made a great effort, stood up, and said firmly, "Until tomorrow!" I accompanied him to the door.

Such nights, such moods do not come twice in one's lifetime. Life would be fine and joyful if such full moments occurred often: then it might even be possible to become reconciled with the idea of death. Nevertheless, I must confess that life is glorious, especially for those who experience it fully, passionately, and warmly; but such people are rare exceptions! What about the masses? They lie in wait at the threshold of our happiness. Those closest to us, connected to us, throw themselves upon us greedily if we acquire even the semblance of happiness, and their pitiless veto hastens to suppress and destroy it in embryo. What about strangers? They, too, keep an eye on us and their slander exposes us to shame. "People, people! Crocodile brood," exclaims one of Schiller's heroes* – I don't know what they really are; but I know they don't sleep or doze; they're always ready to fight, and those bloody battles destroy once and for all any blessing. Sworn enemies of youth, love, and happiness, they persecute and annihilate them inexorably, as if one generation were destined to repay another – as if they lived only for vengeance and rendered as rightful revenge to their successors more than was bequeathed to them by their forebears. They alone ruined my life; but then there is no way to know – perhaps, in turn, I, too, will destroy someone. They say one good turn deserves another – everyone follows that rule without exception, willingly or unwillingly.

The first days of Shrovetide were filled with dances, sleigh rides, breakfasts, and strolls; the last days offered more of the same, and, in addition, masquerades in which even I participated. I didn't pay attention to anyone else but him; he probably didn't see anyone but me; as a result, everyone else saw and noticed only the two of us.

This was inevitable: he was wealthy and distinguished; he'd come from the capital and, suddenly, though surrounded by people of his own circle, he singled out – whom? Who was I? A poor girl! At first everyone was overcome with astonishment: many people didn't believe he could pay so much attention to me except as a joke; but when, during the course of the week, everyone observed the many unmistakable indications of our mutual love – a universal insurrection overtook us, slander enmeshed us, and a storm of indignation was about to burst above our heads. Meanwhile, the two of us, serene, content, and happy, didn't suspect a thing. At last, the general indignation burst into terrible flames, everyone commented loudly on his immorality, my bold impudence, our flouting all convention, irritating decent people, and the extreme shamelessness with which we displayed our bond, as everyone referred to our love. Young women began noticeably to ignore me, their mothers regarded me with proud contempt, while men whispered as I passed by. I didn't perceive much of this very clearly, or else I was so engrossed in my own emotions that I didn't give myself an accurate account of what was happening around me. One fine morning, my stepmother came into my room.

"Antonina," she said to me dryly. "What on earth are you doing? I always knew you didn't know how to behave, but I never thought your shamelessness would reach such a level."

"What have I done?" I asked anxiously.

"What? An amusing question! Ask anyone – they'll tell you. Everyone's saying out loud that you're Michel B***'s lady friend."

I didn't really understand the meaning of that particular phrase, "lady friend." I answered simply:

"What's wrong with that?"

"Are you pretending, or what?" asked my stepmother heatedly. "Or must I use the proper word to describe such things? If you wish – everyone says you're his mistress and that it's a very advantageous profession for a poor young woman, much more profitable than looking after children for a mere thousand rubles a year."

"What do you mean by that?" I asked, my whole body trembling. I sat down in the armchair because my legs started to wobble.

My stepmother noticed the dramatic change of my expression and continued in a somewhat softer vein:

"Be careful: he will have no mercy on you and will abandon you later. That's the usual pattern: men take a liking to a woman, caress her, take her as a lover, and then, when they've had enough, they leave her with contempt. You've ruined your good name."

"No," I replied with indignation. "I don't deserve these words. I haven't done anything, and if anyone should be ashamed, it's those who slander a young woman."

"These are mere words; anyone who provides a pretext for talk must face the consequences: you alone are to blame. If you don't change your behavior from now on, I won't allow you to defame our good name. I will take you back home and force you to behave yourself like a decent young woman – do you hear?"

My stepmother walked out of the room and left me alone, oppressed by horrible, painful thoughts. Doubts crept into my mind, but I suppressed them at once. I was unable to quiet the pounding of my heart at the recollection of his caresses. I was still naive and didn't understand very much – I had always lived alone and had no friends my own age, so where could I pick up the bits of information young maidens usually acquire so easily and share with such great enthusiasm? My thoughts moved quickly; I was frightened by my stepmother's threat to take me home. I knew that Glafira Vasilevna wasn't strong enough to resist and wouldn't think she had any right to oppose my stepmother's wishes; at the first insistent demand, she'd dismiss me from my position.

I got dressed and went into the parlor, having resolved to yield to necessity: so as not to abandon the children, I would distance myself from Michel. When we met, he was surprised by my coldness and my new attitude toward him; after receiving neither a word nor a glance from me all morning, and, seeing that I was avoiding him, he was probably concerned and irritated. He joined a large circle of young women and began paying them compliments; I sat in the corner and watched him say something to Katya Velina; then I saw her smile and flirt with him – this new torment made me heartsick. A young woman otherwise situated in society could assume an indifferent attitude and contend with a rival by displaying her wit among her peers and surrounding herself with new admirers; but I was deprived even of this bitter consolation. I read signs of joy in everyone's eyes at this change in his attitude toward me. I had no one to talk to because hardly anyone would answer me; my social position was beneath everyone's, and now they took advantage of that fact to humiliate me. I was left only to withdraw and keep silent, and so I did. I sat sadly in the corner of the small parlor where the old ladies were playing cards; I began making fretted pictures* for my young ward. My hands were trembling and I didn't know what I felt or how all this had occurred. I was young, extremely ardent, absolutely inexperienced, and therefore concluded that I'd lost Michel's heart and I couldn't endure such an agonizing idea. Besides, laughter and the girls' cheerful conversation and jokes, in the midst of which I could distinguish his voice rising in cheerful tones, constantly landed fresh blows to my heart. All this constituted a completely new torment for me – impotent jealousy completed the picture of my despair. I couldn't endure it, and right after dinner retired to my room and fell onto my bed, and a stream of hot tears flowed from my eyes. Even in my own room I couldn't escape the terrible impression: the sounds, laughter, conversation, and bustle of the young people reached my ears, as if they'd agreed to persecute me, as if they were all enjoying themselves and making merry for the sole purpose of tearing my heart to shreds. I grabbed hold of my head with my hands and buried my hot, teary face in the pillow. Soon I heard Varya's voice in the room next to mine.

"Come here, over here," she said. "I don't know why she keeps on crying."

I glanced up; Michel stood on the threshold, looking at me lovingly. I jumped up from the bed and wiped away my tears. For a few moments we stood there facing each other in silence; he stared at me, sadly, with a gentle reproach and a tenderness in his eyes that overpowered me – I couldn't endure his expressive gaze and lowered my eyes. We were alone: Varya had gone to her younger brother's room.

"Antonina," he said at last and took a step forward.

God knows what was in that sound, that name – inviting, passionate, profound. I know only that it provided a powerful stimulus to my entire being. Apprehension, jealousy, everything was forgotten – once again I believed in him unconditionally. He kissed my hair almost inaudibly and calmed my agitation with half-words brimming with love and tenderness. He led me over to the armchair, made me sit down, and sat next to me.

"Tell me what happened to you today," he said.

I began at once repeating the conversation with my stepmother, softening her words and interrupting the thread of my story with incessant tears.

"Ah, Ninochka, Ninochka!" he said. "Only a week ago you said you weren't afraid of a struggle, and yet the very first signs of it have already broken your spirit."

"No, no!" I cried. "Now I know you love me – go, talk to the others, make jokes, pay them compliments – I'll remain aloof and rejoice in the knowledge that your heart belongs entirely to me – believe me, I'll gladly endure all that awaits me in the future."

"Be sure to remember your promise – have faith in me and don't pay any attention to foolish rumors!"

"Never, never," I replied.

"When will we see each other? I can't stay here much longer: I'm afraid for you and for myself."

"I don't know," I said sadly. "We can no longer talk in the parlor or the drawing room – and there won't be any more dancing."

"Do you know what?" he said. "This evening, after dinner, come to the small gallery in the drawing room – we can chat there."

"I'm afraid," I said timidly.

"Where's your resolution, your strength?" he asked.

"I'm afraid," I replied again unwillingly.

"As you like," he answered. "We don't have long together – yet you're willing to sacrifice our last moments of happiness. It's your own choice – I must submit."

"My God, what can I do?" I asked, crossing my arms, caught between a desire to agree and a desire to refuse him.

"Good-bye," he said. "They're waiting for me in the drawing room to play blindman's buff. If I stay here any longer it would serve as another pretext for rumors and gossip, and that would harm you, not me. Good-bye," he added sadly after a moment's silence, extending his hand to me.

"Good-bye," I replied. "What time should I come to the gallery?"

"After supper," he said, kissing my hands warmly. "Don't be afraid. The gallery's always deserted; you won't be in any danger."

As soon as I was left alone, I was overcome with horror and regretted my promise to meet him later. You don't know how much such a first step really costs: how much suppressed timidity, shame, and terror are aroused in a young woman's heart as she agrees to her first rendezvous. She looks forward to it and fears – what? She herself doesn't know, but she's ashamed and afraid. Men are egotistical – they demand a great deal in the name of their love: they want us to submit gladly, and if they notice that our sacrifice costs us both struggle and effort, they find it as unbearable as a reproach – and gratitude oppresses them like an obligation. If fulfilling their desire doesn't cost us any effort or struggle and the sacrifice is simply offered, they don't appreciate it. But no such thoughts occurred to me at the time. I trembled feverishly all during supper, and, after everyone had dispersed and the drawing room was deserted, with faint heart and a catch in my breath, pausing every few moments, going forward and then taking a few steps back, I proceeded through the corridor and reached the staircase, asking myself why I felt such inner torment and what sort of happiness could possibly redeem this inner rebellion against my own self and this insuppressible fear combined with reproach? At last, inaudibly, quietly, I entered the gallery and found him waiting for me there – he was standing near the entrance, leaning against the wall. Upon seeing me, he rushed to me with an expression of joy and happiness. His impulse frightened me, and I involuntarily retreated a few steps; this fear, a sort of coldness that suddenly replaced my former trustful tenderness and childishly innocent caresses, this fear that made me step back and recoil from his embrace both surprised and irritated him. He came up to me.

"What is it?" he asked with a reproach, "You're afraid, afraid of me? What's the matter? Who has troubled your soul's peace, your youthful innocence? Where did you dredge up this insulting fear? Antonina, don't you trust me?"

"I'm here," I said quietly, "so I must trust you."

He sat me down on a chair and sat at my feet. We talked a great deal, but didn't really say anything in particular; like all people in love, we were preoccupied with each other. If he put his hopes in the future as he had mentioned in our previous conversation, I relied on him alone and placed all my hopes in him. At this meeting, surrounded by the semidarkness of the night, scarcely illuminated by the dim light of a lantern over the staircase, isolated from everyone, sitting next to each other, surrendering ourselves totally to the powerful feeling of mutual love – we were more like children than adults, and if anyone had overheard our intermittent whispering and tender words, he could have easily concluded that we were brother and sister. He was so afraid of offending me, so saddened by my initial display of fear, he loved me so much for my own sake, without any male egoism, that he didn't permit himself a single embrace capable of making me reproach myself for the weakness that had made me come to this rendezvous. We sat there for a long time, oblivious to everything around us. I finally remembered the hour and realized that it was time to return to my room; notwithstanding his pleas, I stood up and, agreeing to avoid meeting in the daytime, I promised to come again some evening. I left, carrying away in my heart both love and redoubled gratitude. I already realized how much I loved him and how defenseless I was: he was my sole protector.

These meetings were repeated rather frequently and ended just as they had to. One night I arrived at the gallery earlier than usual – he wasn't there; soon I heard some footsteps on the stairs, and imagining it was he, rushed to meet him and found myself face to face with Milkot. You recall that the gallery was accessible from another staircase leading to the room occupied by the tutor of my mistress's young nephews. By the horror that immediately took possession of me, I recognized Milkot before I could discern his face in the dim light of the lantern, and froze on the spot like a statue, without thought or movement. We both remained silent for a minute.

"What are you doing here so late at night?" he asked me at last.

I remained silent because I couldn't manage to say a word.

He smiled maliciously.

"Allow me to escort you back to your room," he said, offering me his arm. "Even though you look like a wandering apparition, we're not at the theater. I'd happily laugh it off and tell everyone about this amusing adventure, if I didn't feel so sorry for your stepmother."

He gave me his arm; I didn't take it and rushed to the stairs, but he caught me, and took hold of me with his firm, bony hand, and led me downstairs. When we reached the last step we met Michel; I must have looked terrified because, when he caught sight of me, his face turned pale and he became completely confused – he didn't know what to do. He merely turned aside to let us pass, and, after we went by, he continued upstairs haltingly. Later he told me that he acted as if dazed, went to the gallery, stood there motionless for a long time, and, when he came to, ran downstairs so violently that he woke the servants sleeping in the entry hall. Milkot escorted me to my room in silence, bowed sarcastically, took the key from the door, and was about to leave. I rushed up to him.

"What are you going to do?" I asked.

"I want to eliminate the possibility of any further adventures and wanderings. Do you really think I'll allow you to roam at night – a lovely lady of the darkness?"

I grabbed his arm and tried to snatch the key away, but he squeezed my hand tightly; the pain forced me to release the key at once. Then he shoved me away, left the room, closed the door, and locked it from the outside with the key. The key turned in the lock twice, and its metallic sound dealt me the last blow: I fell feebly into an armchair. Shame, humiliation, and horror took possession of me, as well as fear that a maid who usually came in the morning would find my door locked – all these feelings crowded into my soul and tormented me. I reproached myself for allowing that unfortunate situation to occur – like a madwoman I threw myself down on my knees and cried, "Michel! Michel!" as if summoning him to my aid and putting my last hopes in him. The sound of my own voice brought me back to my senses and restored my ability to think. To what end? In order better to assess my situation and examine the depths of the abyss into which I had carelessly fallen. There was no salvation for me – I knew that. I sat in the armchair and spent the rest of the night sitting there motionless. People had just begun passing through the corridor when the key turned in my lock and my stepmother entered the room. She closed the door behind her.

"This evening you'll kindly say in my presence to Glafira Vasilevna that you're afraid of sleeping alone and wish to move into another room," she said. "I'll invite you to share my bedroom and in that way everything can be arranged without a big commotion. Right after supper you will be so kind as to follow me, do you hear? Also remember that my husband and I, both of us, won't leave you alone even for a minute. You have behaved frivolously long enough and have shamed us – never again! Now get yourself dressed decently and come down to tea in the parlor."

She left the room; I sat there a little longer – then I got dressed and, after washing with cold water, went out to the drawing room. Seeing my stepmother, Milkot, and Michel sitting at the table having tea, my pale face flushed so deeply that Glafira Vasilevna, kissing me as she always did, observed that I looked very attractive and lovely that day.

Lovely! All possible suffering was contained in my soul, and diverse, totally contradictory feelings were tormenting me with incredible force. I was obliged to spend the night with my stepmother; she didn't exchange a word with me, but even her presence at such a painful time, when I wanted to be alone for just a moment or two, oppressed me and added to my suffering. "So there it is, separation," I repeated to myself a thousand times a day and stood like someone struck by lightning at the very thought. I couldn't sleep at all. Two more unbearable days passed like this or almost like this, during which I was watched so vigilantly that I didn't have a free minute and could hardly exchange a single word with Michel.

On the third day Glafira Vasilevna began getting ready to leave for home. Milkot's supervision increased; he almost never left me alone and showed affection in the presence of others, which strained my patience and aroused a painful feeling of impotent rage. I was in a very tense state; while Varya packed her things, I wrote a note to Michel and, slipping it into my pocket, decided to hand it to him no matter what. He was probably planning to do the same; therefore, when we gathered for a farewell breakfast, he sat next to me. Milkot, true to his plan of action, took a place on my other side and constantly chatted with me, joked, and laughed. But all this proved to be in vain. I dropped my napkin intentionally, we bent down together, Michel and I, to pick it up, and managed to exchange notes. When I raised my head, Milkot had fastened a threatening stare on me – he'd obviously guessed everything – but without feeling the least bit afraid, I returned his gaze and, as he poured wine for his neighbor, I hid the note inside the neck of my dress. As soon as we rose from the table, we went to change, say good-bye, and leave. Michel accompanied us to the sleigh – but Milkot also escorted me and, taking my arm, even led me downstairs. Only as I climbed into the sleigh did I manage to squeeze Michel's hand and exchange glances with him – it was impossible to talk, since Milkot was standing beside me.

After our carriage had passed through the gate, Michel caught up with us and, handing our nanny some kind of sack, as if she'd forgotten it, said to me in French:

"You look terrified. Calm down, I beg of you. I'll come to see you very soon!"

"How can I know where I'll be?" I replied. "But wherever I am, remember, I'll always be the same."

Milkot had crossed the courtyard and was just approaching us; Michel cried to the coachman, "Go on!" and turned back. I watched as he met my stepfather and they entered the house together.

What a return! I was traveling along the same route in the same carriage, but had absolutely no recollection of the earlier happy journey. There has been a fair amount of grief in my life, but I always endured it resolutely and often with stoical serenity – but to withstand anxious uncertainty and apprehensions is beyond my power. Slay me at once – I won't complain; tell me my fate – I'll either endure it, reconciling myself, or find some escape, even if, in order to do so, I have to bring ruin upon and even hurt myself. But this terrible uncertainty? Separation, unhappiness, and persecution came upon us so suddenly – we weren't prepared for it. Once again I was in the hands of my inexorable rulers and had to anticipate all possible cruelties at their hands. Was my stepmother's silence an omen of some terrible decision? Of course, I guessed it, but still refused to believe it; the idea that she might take me home to live with them caused me to shudder. Yes, I knew now that my childhood life would be repeated in larger proportions, with broader dimensions – that I'd be delivered entirely into my stepfather's hands, consigned to his unlimited power – that I'd become a passive instrument in his hands – yes, an instrument, because this man, like an executioner, was skilled in all kinds of torture. Once incited to hatred, he knew how to trample the soul of a person entrusted to his care so that nothing whatever would remain alive, so that this person would be disfigured and broken.

When we returned home, I fell dangerously ill. Glafira Vasilevna ascribed my illness to a cold because no one had noticed the drama being played out so unexpectedly among my family, Michel, and myself. She was very alarmed; she sent for the doctor, who came at once and prescribed various remedies, and informed my stepmother, who also lost no time in coming to see me. During my illness she informed Glafira Vasilevna that as soon as I was well again she would take me home because my health was too fragile and my duties with her children were too exhausting. Therefore she was resolved never to part with me again. When I began to recover, I was informed of this decision and told to prepare for the journey home. All of Glafira Vasilevna's entreaties to let me stay went unheeded: I had to obey. During my illness Michel visited us several times; subsequently he told me that he endured indescribable torments at finding himself only three rooms away from me, without being able to enter my room or even to catch a glimpse of me. He even bribed my maid and asked her to admit him just for a moment; but, in spite of her best efforts, she couldn't manage it because I was always under the watchful eye of my stepmother or her maid, who could not be trusted.

I won't describe for you my painful parting with Glafira Vasilevna, her children, and the entire household. Everyone there liked me, and I had grown extremely attached to them. Even Ivan Sidorovich, who, during my entire two-year stay in his house, hardly said more than ten words to me, was deeply moved. Addressing my stepmother, he said with the abrupt kindness of a straightforward Russian man:

"Take good care of her, Madame – see how weak she is. She's a fine girl, she is, with the kindest of hearts!"

As he spoke I smiled bitterly – it seemed that everyone had agreed to mock me, and that he was taunting me when he asked my stepmother to take good care of me.

My days at the Velins passed monotonously, painfully, and infinitely slowly. I settled into my old room, but I brought into it as many agonizing new emotions as the numerous torments that had fallen to my lot. It's a terrible thing, my friends, terrible, to abandon someone you adore without even saying good-bye, weeping on his chest, whispering a few intimate words, giving him one long, last, languorous, dying kiss. I spent days without even moving; my thoughts were concentrated always on one and the same thing – on him, and him alone. Numerous proposals and plans in turn arose and collapsed in my mind; all my thoughts, fixed on one face and image, often resulted in such exhaustion that I'd fall asleep early in the evening, still sitting in a chair. But even during sleep I found no oblivion: the same torments, the same image, persecuted me constantly. My body slept, but my heart was still awake, beating, suffering even in sleep – and I would suddenly awaken, tormented by disturbing dreams. When I lay down in bed again I often had trouble falling asleep for the rest of the night.

Once I was sitting in my room as usual, arms folded, doing nothing in particular, in a total stupor and deep suffering, when my door opened and Alyona, my maid, came in and carefully closed the door behind her. She approached me and silently handed me a note.

I accepted it automatically and opened it, but was unable to read a line; everything grew dark before my eyes. I sat there staring at the beloved, familiar handwriting.

"I was told to wait for an answer," said Alyona.

I came to my senses and began to read. It was one of those letters in which love and tenderness permeate every line and every word, where passion appears in each and every agonizing outburst and insane frenzy. After reading through the whole letter, I couldn't believe my eyes and my good fortune. He was staying as a guest at a neighbor's house and was asking me to meet him in our garden the following day; he set the time, and begged me not to disappoint him and drive him to despair.

I answered him at once. It seemed impossible to refuse. I lacked the strength to do so, and the idea never even entered my head – I would have gone to the ends of the earth for him and after him. I'd begun to take pleasure in the suffering I'd endured for his sake, and joyfully called down on myself all possible persecutions to have the right to feel proud of my love and resolve. My mind had long since matured in its solitude and was now prepared to undertake any heroic feat in order to be united with him. My enterprising audacity, love, and resolve grew stronger with each passing day; fear was the furthest thing from my mind. Indignation with Milkot and my stepmother's stern treatment of me had pushed me to an extreme and forced me to take pleasure at the thought that, in spite of their surveillance and oppressive, humiliating precautions, I would deceive Milkot. Even his fury, if it were out in the open, would arouse only malicious joy and give me even more resolution to overcome all obstacles.

The next day I left the house in late twilight; I walked slowly and carefully with Alyona through the garden and managed to get to the orangery without being seen. I was wearing only a short morning jacket and a warm scarf over my head to hide my face from the servants as I walked past their quarters. My stepmother had long since confiscated my coat and other outdoor clothes as an additional precaution. I lived in such confinement that I couldn't go anywhere without permission; to be absolutely accurate, I couldn't even take a stroll without an escort. In addition, people constantly came into my room to make sure I was there and to see what was I doing.

When he spotted me, Michel was frightened; he wrapped me in his greatcoat and wouldn't let me stay there with him long, saying he'd come only for a moment, merely to bid me farewell since he was leaving for Moscow. We sought ways of corresponding, but were obliged to reject this last consolation; everything we thought of was impossible or infeasible. I was too confined, too surrounded by indifferent or hostile people, and couldn't trust any of them. I had to say good-bye and remain in complete ignorance about how his aunt received the news of our love and his request for her consent to our marriage. He promised he'd write to Glafira Vasilevna, and we invented different phrases to indicate greater or lesser hope of success, based on the results of his conversation with his aunt. After making these arrangements, Michel asked me to return home, begged me to take better care of my poor, precarious health out of love for him, and then said good-bye. Copious, burning tears flowed from our eyes and mingled in our farewell kiss; we both made a great effort and finally tore ourselves away from one another. Do fate and life really bestow such misfortunes? Do people really have to join forces and separate so inexorably and ruthlessly two children, two vital young beings, attracted to one another by invincible sympathy and love?

Upon returning to my room I sat down, exhausted, as if after a long day's march; a terrible, oppressive feeling of loneliness took possession of my soul. At that moment I would have given half my life for one hour of another meeting. If I'd known what was awaiting me, I would, of course, without even thinking, have given my entire life for nothing and died willingly with my unlimited trust in him, in total satisfaction, in the full flowering of my first chaste feeling, still uncrushed, not yet humiliated in my own eyes, with an inviolably pure and unattainably lofty ideal in my soul. Yes, our love was pure and holy; to die then and there – would mean to die like Romeo and Juliet. I don't know of a loftier, more beautiful, splendid death!

》《

She stopped speaking; after a moment's silence that her friends dared not disturb, she continued.

》《

I fell into unbroken despair and hardly left my room. I saw other people only at dinner and tea. I didn't arouse anyone's sympathy or pity; I felt angry all the time at everything around me. My irritability increased and was relieved only by tears in the deep loneliness of my endless solitude. Relations with my stepmother were broken off entirely – we hardly spoke to one another. When we met in the morning, I bowed to her in silence, and she barely acknowledged me with a slight nod of her head. Every time he found an excuse to mock me, Milkot took full advantage of it with pleasure. I usually said nothing and concealed my growing hatred for him behind my contemptuous gaze.

Two months after Michel's departure, Glafira Vasilevna, during one of her visits, told us that Michel had left for Petersburg. That evening I went to see her and, finding her alone, asked permission to read Michel's letter. She agreed to my request immediately and handed it to me. From certain turns of phrase I understood that he'd spoken with his aunt and that we were left with some remote hope; my agitation was so strong that I couldn't control myself, and in a moment my face was bathed in tears. Glafira Vasilevna, in spite of her simplicity and shortsightedness, seemed to understand that we loved each other; upon seeing my tears, she also began weeping and, without a word, without interrogations or rationalizations, embraced me silently and squeezed my hand. Her display of sympathy suddenly eased my soul – I sobbed and threw my arms around her neck. God forbid, my friends, God forbid that anyone should experience such hopeless grief oppressing the soul without someone's tears of sympathy, someone's hand squeezing yours, someone's supportive look speaking directly to your heart. I experienced all this; in that moment the tears of a woman so different in upbringing, intelligence, and morality, a simple, uneducated, but good woman – suddenly infused warmth into my frozen heart, provided fresh energy to my character, and new strength to endure further, probably painful, torments. Yes, sympathy is a great thing, a sacred thing; may God bless thrice all those who provide it sincerely and warmly to a suffering being crushed by life and other people.

All the Velins' children – I'm referring to the youngest – were getting bigger: it was time for their sons to enroll in school. The lessons provided by my stepmother and Milkot were no longer sufficient. It was proposed that in May we would all go to Moscow, where the Velins intended to settle for good to supervise their sons and to introduce Katya, who was already over twenty, into society. My stepmother would have to look for a new post; since Milkot didn't want to live in the country any longer, I began dreaming about liberation. My stepmother found it difficult, almost impossible, to find a position in Moscow with her husband and a step-daughter. The goal of all my hopes was that I might be allowed to work as a governess in someone's household and live apart from my stepmother. At that time I still didn't have that right legally: I was only eighteen and it was a long time before I would come of age. When we arrived in Moscow my stepmother couldn't find an advantageous position and decided to rent an apartment with the interest she received from the small capital she'd managed to save during her years at the Velins. She planned to give music lessons, and her husband would teach languages. They didn't mention me, and I was afraid to raise the question. I lived between two tormenting feelings: fear and hope. I sought out Madame Beillant and asked her to find me a position. She received me very affectionately and amicably, regarding me as a close relative. In spite of our long separation, her best friend's daughter had not become a stranger to her. Perhaps in years gone by she'd loved my father with more than simple friendship, and therefore felt a special tenderness for me. Whatever the case, her chilly relations with my stepmother and their mutual antipathy brought us closer together. At the time I didn't confide in Madame Beillant; subsequently, she heard all about my past and has followed my life ever since; I have no secrets from her. I'm greatly indebted to her.

Milkot rented an apartment and we settled into it; with the help of my stepmother's old acquaintances, lessons gradually increased and our life flowed along a monotonous course. On Sundays my mother often visited the Velins and took me along. You already know that from childhood I didn't like Katya and consequently only set foot in her parents' house against my will. Katya was a lovely, proud, spoiled young lady, who boasted to me of her fine clothes, her numerous conquests, and her suitors. She received me with supercilious affection and a condescending tone of voice, which I could not bear with indifference. My own innate pride had reached an extreme limit and transformed me into a statue whose coldness and immobility often surprised other people in the Velins' parlor. Katya was vain and capricious, but very clever and so quick on the uptake that I couldn't even enjoy the trivial consolation of using her own words to reveal her arrogance with my own acerbic remarks. She didn't allow herself any offensive comments, but something subtly insolent constantly showed through in her treatment of me.

At the beginning of autumn Madame Beillant found me an attractive position and, arranging it with me beforehand, skillfully proposed it to me in my stepmother's presence. She observed that I'd reached the age at which I should be earning my own living, without burdening anyone with extra expenses. My stepmother gave me no chance to reply; she declared definitively that she didn't want me to live in anyone else's household until such time as she was convinced of my moral rehabilitation. I'd already lived with one provincial family, committed more than one foolish act, and managed to bring shame on both her and her husband. Madame Beillant was surprised to hear this; she glanced at me and, noticing the bright blush suddenly spreading across my cheeks, fell silent and didn't raise the issue again. I was staggered by this resolution of my fate – this was a sentence to a life of daily, uninterrupted torment. There was no way out: I had to submit and live under Milkot's hateful roof, without news of Michel, without family or friends. Could I ever find any kindred spirits in this deserted corner of Moscow, which I had no right to leave under any pretext, even to get a breath of fresh air? I lived like a prisoner in the full sense of the word. At least with the Velins, surrounded by family that wasn't my own, their very presence protected me from irony, sarcasm, and insinuations; but now, between Milkot and my stepmother, I was defenseless. In this uninterrupted, daily, trivial struggle my strength began to fade. I became indifferent to everything and endured it all without internal agitation, without heartache – with weariness alone.

Winter and summer passed – and it was autumn. One day I was sitting in the parlor. Milkot wasn't home; he had been off giving lessons all day, and my stepmother, too. Our one servant was also out somewhere. I was all alone, something that rarely happened. Suddenly the bell at the outside door rang loudly. I was startled; a strange premonition gripped my heart. It was now a year since I'd had any news of Michel, except for those few meaningless words I'd managed to hear at the Velins'; I knew only that he still had a post in Petersburg. I stood up and opened the door. Before me stood a young man, a complete stranger.

"What can I do for you?" I asked timidly and despondently.

I don't know why I had hoped that when I opened the door Michel would be standing on the threshold. All my hopes were dashed at the sight of this unfamiliar man; I sadly acknowledged their lack of solid foundation.

"Is this where Mr. Milkot lives?" the young man asked.

"Yes, it is," I replied.

"He and his wife are not at home," he continued so affirmatively that I was surprised.

"That's correct," I said, feeling embarrassed, regretting that I'd opened the door.

"Is Miss Stein at home?" he asked again.

"That's me. What can I do for you?" I said in an astonished voice.

"I recognized you at once," he said. "I asked merely to make absolutely certain. I've come to see you alone. May I come in?"

"No," I said. "Forgive me, but I can't receive anyone."

"I've come from Michel B**," he said with animation.

I cried out.

"I'm his closest friend. I arrived in Moscow a week ago and found you soon afterward, but up to now I couldn't find a convenient time to see you without your servant present. I wanted to find you alone. At last, this morning, I was able to arrange everything and came.

Here's a letter," he added, handing me a large package. "When shall I come for your answer?"

"I don't know," I replied. "Our servant's almost always here. I won't be able to receive you if she's home."

"Don't worry about that. Write your answer and I'll find a way to get rid of her. Good-bye. I don't want to trouble you any longer. Prepare your reply; I'll return in a few days."

I barely managed to utter some incoherent expression of gratitude, closed the door, went into my room, locked myself in, broke the seal, skimmed the letter, and then reread it slowly, pausing over every word, studying each expression, and admiring the handwriting; more than once I began weeping and kissing the dear letter. A year, a whole year, and I hadn't received one line from him; a whole year I hadn't known even a shadow of the least happiness. Now joy of life was streaming into my soul, shedding new light and fresh hope on my sad existence. And he was still the same dear, loving friend. He asked me to be patient; he wrote that neither society, nor work, nor friends had erased my image from his heart and memory: he lived only for me and in the hope of meeting. His friend Dmitry Z** was leaving for Moscow; he asked me to trust him completely, to seek his advice and assistance, and assured me that I would find in him a brother, ready to do anything for our love and happiness. After such a long separation there was not a single word, not one trace of doubt in his letter. His faith in me was just as strong as mine in him.

I wept for a long time after reading the letter and, when I was summoned to dinner, I appeared with eyes red from weeping. My wearied and sad look aroused, as always, an ironic smile and caustic remark from Milkot regarding senseless tears and foolish regrets about something that could never return and was rash to wish for. He added that it was a fitting punishment for my lack of restraint and for yielding to a shameful passion that brought so much righteous censure on my family. I constantly heard such speeches and for a long time responded only with silence, but on that day, it was as if I had derived new strength from Michel's letter, and I objected courageously and coldly. I said that my grief was my own concern and that I could sink into despair from being compelled to endure someone's unbearable presence each and every day. Milkot asked in a threatening way to whom I was referring. I replied without a moment's hesitation that my words referred to him alone. He sent me away from the table and for more than a week my dinner was brought up to my room, which I was not permitted to leave. I would have been almost glad of it if I hadn't seen in such actions a desire to humiliate me and prove that I was no more than a child whom they had the right to punish.

Dmitry Z** returned a week later, having arranged our meetings skillfully and safely. His valet made the acquaintance of our servant, won her over completely with presents and attentions, and entertained her once a week without fail when my stepmother and Milkot were out. During that time I would receive Dmitry Z**. When he found out that I visited the Velins, he made their acquaintance, and I met him there every Sunday and we could talk about Michel. He provided many details about Michel's life in Petersburg and kept telling me that he genuinely loved me. I believed in Michel without question, but still I was delighted to hear confirmation of my hopes and gave myself up to them entirely. Our fate would definitely be decided by the following winter; he was supposed to take his yearly leave, come and talk to his aunt, and demand that she keep her promise. He would remind her that when she said good-bye, she hadn't refused to grant her permission if, as she said, his love was genuine and not a mere outburst of fleeting passion. Next winter would mark the second anniversary of our love, and this constancy in separation, in our opinion, would provide his aunt with incontrovertible evidence of our lasting love. Don't laugh at our confidence –

I was only twenty; Michel and Dmitry, twenty-four. At that age people believe in everything: society's promises, eternal love, will-power that smashes all obstacles to smithereens, and many other foolish things that have no sound basis.

The winter passed more calmly than I expected and provided me several gratifying minutes – namely, when I was talking about Michel or reading his letters. At home I was almost always alone, but I lived in my heart and it blossomed under the warm breath of remote hope. Summer was more boring. Dmitry had to go to the country and, as a result, Michel's and my correspondence was interrupted for three months; Dmitry returned in the autumn and the letters resumed. Then a life full of expectations and anxious longings began. I couldn't get out of bed in the morning without a pounding heart: I was constantly expecting him. I started at the slightest sound, even though I knew he couldn't simply come and visit me; but I was unable to control myself. All this agitation took possession of me without my knowing it, and although I tried to suppress this feeling by thinking logically – it was all in vain.

At last, in November, Dmitry told me that Michel had arrived and would come to see me the next morning. They had some money. Our maid's connection to Dmitry's valet was close and friendly; she'd been handsomely bribed and promised to keep quiet and place her room at our disposal. It was not easy for me to reconcile myself to involving the servants in my intimate affairs and then having to endure their mocking and cunning looks, which remind-ed me so terribly of my hateful dependence on them. Up to this point my maid hadn't suspected anything; now, little by little, the magic circle of deceit was expanding before my very eyes; I was entering it against my will and drawing others after me. I felt humiliated; but inexorable, all-powerful necessity hung over me – I had to choose. I resigned myself and chose temporary humiliation. The door from the maid's room led to the back staircase, by which

Michel and Dmitry could leave at once if my stepmother or Milkot came home and unexpectedly rang at the outer door. The main danger would come if they all happened to meet in the large court-yard of our apartment; but Dmitry was worried about this and never permitted Michel to visit me alone.

How can I describe what I felt the morning after Michel arrived in Moscow? I didn't know what I was doing; I was completely beside myself. More than two years of separation had only strengthened my love for him and given it time to send deep roots into my heart – my life and love merged into one indivisible whole; any damage to my love would result in my own demise. I existed only by thinking of him and the strength of our mutual attachment. My soul enjoyed such a bright holiday! I was reborn and relished the fullness of my young, passionate life, the abundance of love and youth. I was hap-pily agitated; blood coursed through my veins and impetuously flooded my trembling heart. Like a child, I entered the room vacat-ed by the maid and set about sweeping her poor floor and wiping the dust from the table; when everything was tidy, I returned to my own room. I began dressing and let down my curls *à l'anglaise,* a style he had always admired; after finishing these preparations, I sat down in my chair, but couldn't remain there quietly. I wandered from room to room, glancing out of the frosty windows, from which, however, it wasn't really possible to see our entrance. I smiled through my tears and tried to suppress this agitation mixed with fear and joy. At last the bell sounded; I felt a surge in my heart and rushed like lightning, but not to meet him: I no longer had con-trol of myself and didn't know what I was doing. I ran into our maid's room and sat down on a chair, scarcely drawing breath. I don't recall how many minutes I sat there waiting; at last I heard the maid's voice. She said:

"This way, please. Here's my room."

The door opened and Michel's tall figure appeared on the threshold. I cried out, and then, without words or tears, came to my senses with my arms wrapped around his neck. He carried, not led, me to the chair and sat down quietly next to me. We gazed at one another for some time without saying a word, without moving a muscle, our hands squeezed tightly together. At last, with sobs choking me, I buried my head on his shoulder; a stream of tears gushed from my eyes and relieved my restricted breathing. I cried for a long time; he kissed my hands and also wept. After the first broken words of reunion, of questions posed without waiting for answers, of incoherent conversation interrupted a thousand times by caresses and exclamations of joy in which one beloved name was constantly repeated – in short, after the expression of these chaotic impulses of the soul in the presence of a much-beloved, long-awaited friend, which all of us have experienced at least once in life – we both calmed down. I looked around and saw Dmitry Z** standing by the closed door, protecting us from unforeseen dangers. His face expressed so much sympathy that I said to him:

"Come here and sit down next to us – you won't interfere. Share our happiness. Aren't you our friend and brother?"

He came over and sat down.

"Listen, my friends," he said some time later, interrupting my conversation with Michel. "I've been listening to you for more than half an hour. You're simply wasting time. You know you can't see each other often. Now you must talk about important matters; later on you can chat as much as you like about whatever you wish."

"Let us be," said Michel. "Let me look at her! I haven't seen her in two years. Two years: that's terrible! I can't believe I'm here with her."

"Listen," said Dmitry. "You must try to bring all this to an end. Consider our position: we have to depend on a maid, but can't trust her too far. Do you want to subject Antonina Mikhailovna to new grief?"

"God forbid!" said Michel. "She's gone through enough already.

I merely want to postpone the discussion of important matters until our next meeting. Now I want to look at her and tell her how much I love her."

"No, no!" said Dmitry. "Tomorrow you have to talk to your aunt. You must take advantage of her initial delight at seeing you again to press your demand for her consent."

"Yes," I said. "Let our fate be decided. I can't live with the thought that this should all come to light. I can no longer live in dependence on others, much less a maid. Besides, better unhappiness than uncertainty."

"Why unhappiness? My aunt has always loved me dearly. Can she really remain intransigent? Oh, no! I have hope," said Michel.

"All the more reason for speaking to her without delay," said Dmitry.

"So you both want me to do this," said Michel, looking at the two of us. "I will speak with her tomorrow."

I detected the extreme tension in his voice. One might conclude that he'd gladly agree to postpone for a while this discussion with his aunt; he'd resolved to do it knowing both how difficult it was and how timid he was. I squeezed his hand and burst into tears.

"But remember, Ninochka," he said. "Nothing in the world will part me from you. Don't cry, my dear."

"I know that," I replied. "I'm only crying because I feel sorry for you. It's hard for you to speak with your aunt."

Dmitry glanced at him and said simply:

"Assurances are unnecessary; you've both endured too much. You're too attached to one another for anything to come between you. If your aunt doesn't agree to your marriage, if she reneges on her near-promise, we'll have to arrange it some other way."

"What are you trying to say?" I asked, frightened.

"Why specify in advance? We'll see soon enough," he replied. "Now it's time. Let's go."

"One more minute," said Michel.

"It really is time," objected Dmitry. "They could find us here, and you certainly don't want to exclude the possibility of meeting again." Michel stood up.

"Good-bye, Ninochka," he said. "I'll be back in three days."

"No, wait a bit," I said, getting up as if I wanted to hold him there.

He took me by both hands and stared at me as if trying to etch the features of my face in his mind and carry them away in his memory. I became embarrassed and turned pale.

"Antonina Mikhailovna," said Dmitry. "Be sensible, be strong. You'll see him soon, I give you my word. But now it's time to go. I'm afraid for you."

"Good-bye, my friend. Good-bye, Michel," I said, squeezing his hands, which I still didn't want to release.

He went down on his knees before me and kissed both my hands; looking deep into my eyes, he left the room quickly and then turned back once more.

"Make the sign of the cross over me," he said. "I'm afraid. Tomorrow will decide our fate. I believe that your blessing will bring me luck."

I crossed him and, taking his head in my hands, I kissed his delicate, soft hair; once again tears flowed from my eyes.

"Enough," said Dmitry. "Are you really only children, and not adults? It is we ourselves who arrange our fate; others have no power over it if we don't give it to them. Why are you parting with such anguish, as if it's forever?"

"How do we know?" I said.

He took Michel's arm, and soon I heard their steps as they quickly descended the back staircase. Scarcely had I managed to return to my room when I heard the bell again; the door opened and Milkot walked into my room. I realized that Dmitry Z** had saved us and that our meetings would certainly have ended with the first, had it not been for his prudent intervention. This idea so frightened me that I looked at Milkot with timidity and embarrassment.

"What's wrong with you?" he asked me insolently. "You know, I'm really beginning to think you're not always in your right mind. Sometimes you look as if I wanted to cut your throat. Why do you look so dazed? This would all be very amusing if I weren't so fed up with it."

I was silent and sat there without raising my eyes; my heart was so full of a different emotion that I paid no heed to his words. Seeing that I had no answer, he continued:

"When will you stop playing the part of a victim? If you were to do something, it would be better than sitting here with your arms folded or wandering from room to room like a ghost. Admit that you can't really pretend to be a victim, when you live so comfortably and idly on money earned by other people."

"I'm living here against my will," I said. "Let me go find a position."

"Yes, so you can make a fool of yourself. We know all about you! We've already seen what it means to let you live alone. You brought us considerable disgrace in the province of T***."

I left the room in silence, and he went to his own room. The next day I received a note from Michel. It was incoherent and consisted of only a few lines: he wrote that he'd tell me everything at our next meeting. I realized that there was little hope; all that day I sat in my room, in the anguish of expectation and with a presentiment of new misfortunes. I waited for him in vain for three days; fortune had never smiled on me – and so it was during those days. My stepmother and Milkot were always at home; they didn't go anywhere because of the holidays. On the evening of the third day my stepmother proposed a visit to the Velins. Concealing my joy, I agreed to go. I hoped to find Dmitry there and was not disappointed in my expectation. Many guests were present at the Velins that day. They'd gathered for an informal dance to piano music. Dmitry invited me to dance and, while we executed a quadrille,* said:

"I have a great deal to tell you now. I came here primarily to see you."

"Tell me quickly," I replied with an impatient gesture.

"Listen, Antonina Mikhailovna. I've brought some not very consoling news, but everything can still be remedied. You must be firm and decisive."

"My God!" I said, my expression changing. "Tell me, tell me at once! Don't torture me."

"If you behave like this, you'll just draw everybody's attention. I'm afraid to tell you. Calm down first."

"I am calm," I said firmly, making an effort to control myself. "I can guess it all: his aunt didn't give consent."

"She didn't even want to hear about it!" he replied.

I recoiled involuntarily; no matter how prepared I was for this blow, it still overwhelmed me with its force. We both fell silent for a few minutes.

"How could she have promised two years ago?" I asked, interrupting the silence.

"Just so; she thought it was a childish whim, a passing fancy. But, after his return, when he began to insist on obtaining her consent, she declared decisively that she'd never allow him to marry you."

"That means it's all over," I said with suppressed desperation.

"Not at all," he replied. "You must simply be firm. There's still a way. In my opinion, there's always a way if we're not senseless enough to destroy ourselves. Listen to me carefully. Michel's a splendid fellow, kind and noble, with the tender heart of a woman. But his character contains the terrible seed of all sorts of unhappiness: he's weak-willed and compliant. I know his aunt. He'll never have the resolve to tell you, and I've remained silent to this point, but now I'll tell you everything, in order to save you both. His aunt is a withered, inflexible, resolute old woman: she's always exerted great influence over him. He's simply afraid of her and lacks the strength to oppose her: not now, of course, not at the very first moment of outrage and suffering, but afterward, *à la longue*. He'll be terribly unhappy because he loves you passionately and sincerely, and yet, in spite of all that, he'll submit to his aunt's influence without fail. You must save him and yourself."

"But how?" I asked. "You surprise me. I always thought his aunt loved him inordinately."

"Yes, indeed she does; but there are quite a few people on earth who love in a very strange way, under certain conditions, more for themselves than for those they love. Don't you know what prejudice is all about? Michel entered this struggle carelessly, without taking anything into consideration, under the influence of his first real attachment. But this struggle will be beyond his strength: he won't withstand it if you don't support him. If you leave him to his own devices or consign him to his aunt's control, she'll demolish both of you."

"You're destroying me," I said. "What can I do? I have no power when faced with this."

"Not at all. On the contrary, you're stronger than anyone else. Michel loves you more than anyone in the world; he's ready to do anything for you. Give him the will; don't do anything to discourage him. On the contrary, give him strength."

"You're not being clear. Explain yourself," I said.

"He wants to carry you off and marry you in secret."

"My God!" I said. "Is it really possible?"

"Why not? It's altogether possible. In three or four days everything will be ready. Nobody will grieve over you: nobody at home loves you. It's the only way out. You must take it. Later, perhaps, even if you wanted to, it will be too late. Honestly, listen to me. We'll come tomorrow to hear your answer."

I stood in silence, staggered by this proposal; I was confused, my head was clouded, and I couldn't think it out. My gaze, wandering aimlessly and mechanically around the room, inadvertently fell upon the door. A tall, heavy woman, massive and theatrically majestic in appearance, walked into the room; her eyes and hair were black, her nose, large and aquiline, her brows, straight and sharp, her lips, compressed. She reminded me of a portrait of Lady Macbeth. Michel came in behind her.

"Who's that?" I asked in instinctual fear, taking Dmitry's hand.

"That," he said, "is Michel and his aunt."

"We're lost," I replied. "That woman has neither soul nor heart. Nothing will touch her, nothing will mollify her – I'm sure of that."

"Ah! At last you understand. Yes, it's really true. And, if you remember that Michel is totally in her hands, you can gauge the full depth of your misfortune."

"You're cruel," I said. "Why do you torture me? What have I done to you? I've loved you and still do."

He took my hand and squeezed it.

"Don't you see I'm trying to help you?" he said. "I'm saving you in spite of yourselves. Look at that stony countenance, read all that threatens you there, and decide for yourself! Do you really want to shatter your life against that granite cliff?"

Dmitry spoke with malicious irony. I glanced at him with an imploring look. He changed his tone and added:

"Rely on me. I'll arrange everything, but you must give your consent."

The quadrille ended. Catching sight of Michel B**, my stepmother came looking for me and wanted to leave immediately, but the mistress of the house prevailed upon her to stay, saying that they were short one couple for two quadrilles. Then my stepmother came over to me and said sternly that I should control myself and behave properly if I didn't want to be locked up at home for the rest of the winter. Michel saw me, came over, and bowed; after exchanging a few meaningless words, he walked away and apparently paid me no more attention. He danced several waltzes with Katya, who flirted with him the entire evening. A quadrille was begun; by chance, my partner and I stood opposite Michel's aunt, who was sitting in a row of elderly ladies and watching the dancers. She raised her lorgnette to take a good look at me and, turning around, gestured to Katya, who was gliding past in a figure of the quadrille. Katya ran up to her graciously and politely, greeted her, and, after saying a few words, returned to her partner. I don't know why, but I thought Madame B** had asked who I was, and, when she began to examine me with a quite insolent curiosity, checking me over from head to toe without lowering her gaze, I was absolutely convinced of the truth of my supposition. I blushed under the weight of her leaden gaze and was happy when the quadrille ended and we could leave. My stepmother was probably pleased by my cool behavior toward Michel because she didn't say one harsh word to me on the way home. Both she and my stepfather were far from thinking that I had any dealings with Michel. They naturally assumed this bit of youthful mischief had long since been forgotten. The time was nearing when I would be free of them and find a position in another household as a governess. At the present time, however, my thoughts were moving in a different direction; all my hopes and desires were fixed on my conversation with Dmitry.

The next morning Michel and Dmitry came to see me.

"My dear," Michel said to me sadly, "yesterday Dmitry told you there's no hope for us. My aunt doesn't even want to hear about our love. All is lost! But I've decided that I must save you from this terrible life you are suffering because of your love for me. For my part,

I can't live without you, either. I want to take you away from here, marry you in secret, and keep you hidden until everything is sorted out between me and my aunt. Will you agree?"

I was silent.

"My dear, my Antonina, don't ruin our happiness. Give your consent – I beg you, I implore you! Can you really pronounce the terrible verdict condemning me to a life of loneliness and yourself to eternal torment? Give your consent – I implore you!"

"Antonina Mikhailovna," said Dmitry, "remember everything I told you yesterday and take pity on Michel. If you don't agree to his proposal, he'll have to engage in an open, overt struggle with his aunt. He will be faced with persecution. You know what it's like from experience; you've borne it yourself. It's not easy, is it?"

"He's a man," I said. "He can't be victimized like a woman."

"That's true. But remember, your own heart has hardened against the people you live with, whereas he still loves his aunt and owes her everything. She raised him. His father will also side with her. Michel will suffer twice as much. But if he's already married – then, in her opinion, it will be an irrevocable misfortune. Believe me, she'll forgive him, if not immediately, then very soon; but, until it's all settled, she's sure to persecute both of you. If you don't pity yourself, then at least take pity on him."

"Do you have the right," asked Michel heatedly, "the right not to consent and to hesitate? Why? In your opinion have we not suffered enough? Are we suffering too little now? Haven't we both earned the right to be happy? My God, who can be bothered by our happiness? Or do you love me less now? Remember what you told me two years ago; remember what you repeated in your letters. You assured me you'd be firm and resolute. Prove your love for me – the time has come."

I rushed to him and burst into tears.

"Take me away from here," I cried. "Do as you wish!"

He squeezed my hand warmly and firmly. Dmitry, exultant, kissed my hand; all during this scene, it seemed to me that he played a larger role than Michel and rejoiced for all of us. After that, they left quickly, while I, as befits my own strange nature, suddenly felt calm; returning to my room, I spent the day reflecting on the situation. My fate was decided, my word had been given. Thinking everything through again, I felt reconciled and justified in my own eyes, acknowledging my inalienable right to choose a husband I loved, completely convinced that I wasn't ruining Michel. On the contrary, I was rescuing him from the painful consequences of his love for me that would ensue once he was engaged in a desperate, overt struggle with his entire family – I knew that he could never give me up.

The next day I began to prepare, as if for a journey. Putting a few things aside, I first packed the portrait of my father – my single treasure – and then the small box that had belonged to him in which I kept Michel's letters. In addition, I chose two dresses and a few personal items. Wrapping everything together, I hid the bundle under my bed. I fell asleep late, thinking about my father; most likely, it was my agitated imagination that occasioned the dream that so troubled me upon awakening. I saw my father: he appeared pale and sad, just as on the night before his death. Twice he said my name, calling me. I struggled between a desire to follow him and a desire to remain behind for Michel, whom I was expecting. My father summoned me several times and finally disappeared, moving down a winding road. I rushed after him and suddenly found myself amid a desert and quicksand. I was completely alone and feeling very tired, but I advanced indomitably under the burning sun and stifling heat. I looked everywhere for my father but couldn't find him. My energy exhausted, I tried to return home but couldn't find the way out. I awoke exhausted and sighed deeply as I escaped this painful nightmare. Don't be surprised that I recount it to you. I've always been superstitious and, in my opinion, this dream, portending some inescapable grief, came close to influencing my fate. After awakening, I had less hope for the success of our undertaking. It seemed to me that some chance occurrence would certainly impede us. Don't laugh. All women are impressionable and readily surrender to premonitions, and I more than most. But I tried hard to dissuade myself; by the next day all traces of the dream had vanished from my memory. I sat in my room waiting for news. At noon I received a brief note from Dmitry. He wrote:

"Everything's ready. Tonight at eleven o'clock proceed down the back stairs. You'll find me at the gate."

I shuddered involuntarily, but then gained control of myself and calmly went downstairs for dinner. My stepmother, for some strange reason, treated me with greater affection than usual; that is, she even chatted with me, while Milkot hadn't a single unpleasant word for me. Afterward I returned to my room at once, feeling that my resolve might weaken, and I was secretly indignant at that fact. You may ask how I could possibly feel sorry for my stepmother and Milkot. Well, I didn't feel sorry for them; I merely felt that, at the moment of parting, I could forgive them sincerely for everything in the past, the long suffering of my childhood and youth. I was furious with myself for this inability to suppress my emotions. Involuntary tears welled up in my eyes when I compared my fate with that of other women who, at the time of their marriages, surrounded by the love of family, companions, and friends, and deluged with blessings, move peacefully to plight their troth with their sweethearts. I felt my loneliness deeply and sadly. I sat silently in my room waiting for the appointed hour. Thoughts wandered aimlessly through my mind, and my heart pounded even more randomly. At this critical moment of my life I experienced an involuntary trepidation. I tried to concentrate on the happiness awaiting me, but I thought about other things. At about nine o'clock the maid came into my room and handed me a letter. The handwriting didn't look familiar; I tore open the seal feverishly and, reading it through in haste, was stunned. I've kept that letter, my friends, and will read it to you now:

"Dear Madam: I learned only a week ago that you are the one who is the object of my nephew's love. I don't know and have no desire to discover the means by which you enticed him into such an insane, impossible liaison. I'm writing merely to say that all your efforts are absolutely futile. I will never give my consent or blessing to his marriage to you. I advise you to abandon all your designs, especially since it's disadvantageous for you to persevere. It's true my nephew is wealthy, but that's only because I, after taking the place of his mother, my sister, have spared no expense on his behalf up to this point. If he were to decide to disobey me and my wishes, I will deprive him of his inheritance and transfer all my wealth to his two sisters. I don't know if you have a fair impression of my character: let me state simply that I am not among those aunts and uncles in plays who are moved by the entreaties of lovers or spouses, who forgive them their premeditated and intentional crimes, and who, at the moment of reconciliation, hasten to confer on the young couple all their wealth together with their blessings. I never forgive. His father will follow my example. Consider then: What good is it for you to marry a man who'll always be poorer than a suitor of your own class? At least any such man would possess knowledge and skills and, having been born to labor and poverty, could guarantee a life for himself and his family. My nephew was raised as the heir to my estate; he has the knowledge he needs, but is in no position to convey it to others, even to give lessons. And, even if he were capable of it, judge for yourself: What would become of a man so used to living in luxury who suddenly falls into the extreme destitution you cannot escape? In addition, my curse, and his father's as well, will fall on his guilty head and tear his heart out. If you really love him, you must save him from ruin. Nor should you forget that he's a civil servant,* and marrying without consent is less possible for him than for others. All your ambitious designs will be crushed by bitter reality; I can predict all sorts of misfortunes for you in the future. Perhaps my letter won't dissuade you, but I warn you that I will follow your every action indefatigably. And if you, carried away by unrealizable hopes, decide to oppose my will and attempt to infringe on my right to arrange my nephew's fate, a duty with which I was entrusted by his late mother, if you ever encourage him in any reckless venture, I shall seek legal redress. Believe me: any attempt on your part will be futile and not without risk for you. Don't force me to take decisive action with the assistance of my numerous connections and prominent relatives; I can have you permanently banished from the city, together with your stepmother and her husband. I would have written to her, but I considered that totally unnecessary. I know you are acting against your stepmother's orders and often ignore them. Now you have been warned. I have now discharged my obligation with regard to you; if you choose to bring misfortune upon yourself, you will have only yourself to blame."

I sat there for a long time, like a statue, my gaze fixed on those terrible words. Then I stood up and, with the calm of hopeless despair, took out the bundle I'd prepared the evening before, unfastened it, and, unpacking all my things, returned them to their previous place in the wardrobe. When I took out my white dress, I was suddenly overcome by a fit of wild laughter so close to madness that it frightened me. It took sheer force of will to break it off. At that moment my eyes fell upon the portrait of my father, which I was holding, preparing to put it back in place. His calm, quiet face looked at me meekly; I fell to my knees involuntarily, pressed my face against his, and a bitter, unending stream of tears came pouring forth from my eyes. When I came to my senses, the clock was just striking half past eleven. I hurriedly threw on my light jacket and ran down the back stairs. Dmitry was waiting for me at the gate.

"Let's go, it's past time. I was beginning to be afraid that something had happened to you," he said hurriedly.

"I'm not going anywhere," I replied firmly. "Tell Michel that he's free."

Dmitry was dumbfounded and took a few steps backward.

"What are you saying?" he asked.

I repeated my words.

"Antonina Mikhailovna, what do you mean?" he asked heatedly. "Good Lord, isn't it a sin to mock the person you love? Yes, and it's a sin to toy with both of your lives!"

"I've only just come to my senses. I was on the edge of an abyss and, realizing that, I halted – that's all there is to it."

"Tell me what all this means. I thought you were a decisive woman, but you're worse than a child, and weaker, too."

I smiled.

"Listen," I said. "I just received a letter from his aunt. She's threatening both me and him with her curse and swears to deprive him of his inheritance and leave him in poverty forever."

"So what? He can work and so can you. If you have a head on your shoulders and two strong arms, you'll never die of hunger."

"He's not accustomed to working; he grew up in luxury and has no idea of poverty – it'll kill him. His aunt also writes that she'll resort to the law if he marries me."

Dmitry was silent for almost a minute. Then he replied:

"To do so she'll have to submit a petition against her nephew and ask that he be punished. She'll never do that."

"And if she does? I can see from her letter that she's capable of anything," I said.

"What of it? He'll endure persecution out of his love for you. He himself has said more than once that happiness is possible only with you."

"No! We would have to endure too much. I have no way to repay him for so many sacrifices. What? Losing his fortune and a career, invoking his relatives' hatred and his beloved father's curse – not for anything on earth!"

"But he's waiting for us. What will I tell him?" Dmitry continued insistently. "How can I go to him alone? He'll never endure this blow just when he has hope."

I felt so sad at hearing those words that my resolution weakened. I burst into tears, imagining vividly Michel's grief when he learned of my decision. Dmitry saw the impression his words had made and tried to take advantage of this moment of deep emotion. He took my hand and tried to guide me out to the street. I stopped.

"Listen," I said. "My decision is final. I'm sacrificing myself for his happiness. It's my duty. Don't say a thing: your words will go in one ear and out the other and have no effect on my decision."

"It's an insane sacrifice," said Dmitry warmly. "I'll run and fetch Michel, bring him here, and we'll see how your cruel intention to tear yourself away from him stands up when you see his despair."

"No, no!" I said. "Why this new torment? My God! My God! Enough suffering, enough!"

But he wasn't listening to me any longer. He rushed from the courtyard and disappeared beyond the gate. I stood on the same spot for several minutes; then, feeling unsteady, went back upstairs to my room. So that was the end of my staunch resolve to become his wife. There it is, the first evidence that we're governed by the play of fate, and willpower is no more than a childish dream that charmingly seduces the inexperienced. If only his aunt's letter had come later! When, after receiving it, I kissed my father's portrait with such insane passion, I already knew that I was all alone in the world left only with his memory, and that I had lost my one true friend forever, my dearest beloved. It was very painful, but I didn't hesitate for a moment. Up to the present no one can make me act in a way different from what the innermost feeling I recognize as genuine demands; it alone has never deceived me! I sacrificed myself completely, but my sacrifice proved to be superfluous. Subsequently, I learned that Michel was so distressed and confused on the day designated for our elopement that he'd aroused his aunt's suspicion. She began keeping an eye on him, summoned his valet, and, eliciting a partial confession from him, went to see her nephew at the very moment he was leaving his room on the way to meet me. Their conversation began heatedly; it soon became terribly angry on her part and manifestly indignant on his. I don't know why, whether by calculation or simply by chance, but she suddenly burst into tears and threw her arms around him. Her pleas disarmed him entirely – he didn't know how to oppose them and was unable to. He was defenseless and weak when confronted by them. Then she felt faint: her illness was the final blow, and put an end once and for all to his will and demolished his resolve.

The next day I received a note from Dmitry. He wrote that Michel refused to leave his aunt's bedside, that the evening before he wouldn't even receive Dmitry, and that day he could only see him for a few minutes alone. He added below in a postscript, which clearly displayed his stalwart and decisive character, that I shouldn't be concerned about the health of Madame B***; knowing that I was capable of some foolish act, he gave me his word that the attacks of nerves she was having were not in the least dangerous, and that every rational person knows that a first episode doesn't mean very much, especially in women. They are able to produce symptoms intentionally by willing them. After reading this letter, I sank into dull despair and a complete collapse of spirit and strength; I suffered my first real illness, which not even Dmitry could laugh off. Our doctor, called by my stepmother against my will, prescribed medicines of some sort and repeated more than once that they would have no effect if I did not remain calm in spirit and protected from shocks. My stepmother was surprised and replied that I hadn't experienced anything of the sort recently. The doctor shook his head in disbelief and asked under what circumstances I'd fallen ill. When he was told that my illness had come on suddenly and completely unexpectedly, he shook his head, repeated his words once more, and left, promising to return soon. My illness lasted six weeks, and during that time I didn't see anyone. Occasionally I received letters from Michel. He didn't say anything in particular – there was no mention of plans or hopes; he merely assured me that he loved me as much as ever, complained bitterly at our oppressive fate, mourned our separation, and, informing me about his aunt, always added that her health was extremely poor and she'd yet to recover from the terrible shock she'd suffered.

At the same time an important change occurred. Dmitry's father sent him to Petersburg to attend to some serious business affecting half of their estate; thus was I deprived of a friend and his assistance. This last circumstance definitively altered my fate and led to many new misfortunes for me. I wept bitter tears when I said good-bye to him.

Don't rebuke me, don't judge me harshly, don't accuse me of weakness – actually I never in my life, neither before nor after, cried as much as I did during this transitional epoch in my existence. Tears became my normal condition; a feeling of my own impotence, my complete reliance on other people, destroyed any moral independence in me. There was not even a hint of resilience; I lay in a passive, indifferent state with no attempt to escape and found relief only in tears. And what else could I do? Hostile surroundings, the cruel determination of Michel's relatives, his own weakness, and the might of our persecutors imposed an indestructible burden on us; I could merely bend under its weight. I abandoned all hope and made no further attempt to throw off the yoke. Dmitry, saying good-bye, had no hope either; he squeezed my hand sadly and said merely that I would continue to receive Michel's letters through one of their mutual acquaintances, Vasily N**.

"More strangers," I said with exhaustion. "Why must we keep on involving other people? Michel feels no pity for me," I added, offended at the ease with which he turned to new people to maintain our relations, as if he himself couldn't come to see me.

"There's nothing else he can do," Dmitry explained. "His aunt won't let him leave her. He can't even trust his own valet, who's already betrayed us once. Besides, Michel's no longer receiving any money and soon he won't even be able to pay for such services. Vasily N**'s an honest man and told me you know his sister well."

"Yes," I said. "I've seen her at the Velins'. She's a nice girl."

I bowed to necessity. Our affairs were not progressing; winter passed monotonously, and I gradually recovered from my illness. Sometimes I saw Michel: he dropped in when he could tear himself away from his aunt's house and I was home alone. We noticed great changes in each other – he and I had fallen into a state of dull hopelessness. He didn't delve into the details of our unsuccessful escape, but merely alluded to it in passing; nor did he discuss the circumstances of his life at home. Assuring me of his love, he occasionally mentioned hope for the future, but it was obvious that he did so to console me and didn't believe it himself. This was not real life – it was agonizing torment. He didn't have the strength of will to reject me, much less to find a way out of our painful predicament. His tenderness toward me remained constant; at our meetings he was just as affectionate and loving, but I realized how impotent and exhausted he was, even though he assured me of the opposite and often asserted, as if to comfort himself and me, "It can't get any worse!" We both were aware of how much fate and other people threatened us: he had given in to them, and I could resist no further. We were both weary, he more than I. He didn't talk about what was happening at home; but from his gloomy look, I could conclude that he was being subjected to persecution or entreaties. Subsequently, I learned that both were applied and tormented him equally. I didn't want to wrest a confession from him. My own situation became more painful and difficult by the day; I felt, even though I didn't admit it to myself, that the support I got from his presence was growing noticeably weaker every day and gradually disappearing. Once I even proposed that we end our relationship and give in completely to the people who were trying to keep us apart. This suggestion, made so abruptly and firmly, distressed him and aroused him from the moral lethargy into which he had sunk. All of a sudden he rebelled heatedly, reproached me for my weakness and loss of hope, reminded me of all our promises and oaths, and mercilessly accused me of not loving him any more. This fiery burst of passion totally disarmed me; I was ashamed of my lack of faith, reproached only myself, begged him to forgive me, and swore never to doubt him again.

"If I'm sad, Ninochka," he said to me gloomily, "it's only because my heart is broken. I stand between two very powerful attachments – my insane love for you and the affection and gratitude I feel for my aunt. What's to be done? To complete our unhappiness, she's been warned about you and often repeats that if . . . "

He stopped.

"Go on," I said, "if . . . "

"I don't know how to tell you. She's heard some strange rumors – she's been told you have a strange character – that you're willful and frivolous."

"No doubt," I said, "Katenka Velina or her mother did me that service."

"Oh, no! I don't think so. More likely it was Liza N**. You used to see her at the Velins', and she visits our house. Katenka says she's sly."

"That's not true," I said. "But never mind that. So everyone knows about our relationship?"

"Oh, no!" he said with embarrassment. "My aunt," he continued, returning to the previous topic, "can't understand that I genuinely love you; she thinks I'm merely infatuated. All the blame lies in that error: it's not pride or arrogance that makes her oppose our marriage, merely her misgivings about my future happiness with you."

I shook my head sadly.

"Don't you trust me? You've reached the point of doubting everything, but you have no right to do so. You don't know my aunt, so why don't you trust me? What have I done to deserve this? Haven't I taken all possible steps? Chance alone has thwarted our intention."

"And my will," I said proudly, recalling his aunt's letter, which I hadn't shown him.

"What does that mean?" he asked.

"It means," I replied with feeling, but avoiding a full explanation and already regretting what I'd said, "it means that I love you more than anything on earth and am prepared to make every possible sacrifice for your happiness."

"I know, I know, I believe – I believe you, but – why don't you trust me?"

"I do, my friend," I said in a heated burst of emotion that made me repudiate my previous words and doubts only because his gaze was so filled with love and sadness. "The future will show how strong my faith is. Your words will be my law, my reason; even if the whole world were to rise up and bear witness against you, rest assured, I won't believe it."

We looked at each other tenderly and our union was forged even more tightly than before – at least that's what I thought at the time.

The young heart has to suffer many blows before it ceases to trust; the young mind must endure many betrayals before it can grasp that such things are possible; the very being must withstand many powerful shocks before it splits into two parts, one preserving the love while the other debates whether the object of its love is really worth loving. During the first stage of life, love, devotion, and self-sacrifice constitute a single unbreakable whole, and we are given over entirely to the person we love. Reason remains silent; there's not even a seed of analysis of oneself or others. The festering sore of analysis that destroys every feeling at its source has yet to come into existence; it appears unexpectedly, after the first storm, shattering young life, and, manifesting itself in us, it breaks into our memory of the past and examines every last petty detail of it. That's the first thing. Later, having stolen into our soul, this destructive impulse settles down there, developing gradually and growing to monstrous proportions. It mercilessly destroys forever the life of the heart by never admitting into it any vital sensations. Analysis, like the anatomist's knife, cuts through and destroys vital energy everywhere, leaving behind a corpse where only a moment before blood was flowing, life was throbbing, and a heart was beating. At that time I still didn't know that kind of analysis, that terrible, destructive malady; its absence caused in part the blow that severed the bond between me and Michel. Now it remains for me to tell you all about it.

Winter came to an end and it was Lent. On the Sunday of Shrovetide, my stepmother received a note from Madame Velina insisting that she come to see her, saying she had something very important to communicate. My stepmother dressed hurriedly and set off; about an hour and a half after her departure I heard her return and go straight in to see my stepfather, without even going into her own room next to mine. I was sitting very calmly in my room when the door opened and my stepmother came in; she was pale and her angry expression startled me. I was even more surprised when

Milkot followed her in and locked the door. He'd never set foot in my room before. I found his presence somewhat disconcerting.

"Michel B***'s letters," my mother said to me, her voice trembling.

I looked at her without understanding a thing.

"I'm asking you for Michel B***'s letters," she repeated with growing fury.

"I can't give them to you," I said finally, in a decisive tone. "They were written to me."

"All right!" she said. "I'll find them myself."

She quickly approached the small table and picked up my box.

"They're in here," she said, addressing Milkot. "This was her father's box – I know they're in here. The key!" she demanded abruptly, "or I'll break the lid."

I was wearing the key to the box around my neck.

"It's true," I said, standing up. "It's true: hatred is equal to love. You've guessed correctly. His letters are in there, but I won't give you the key. Will you really break open your late husband's box, the one he got from his mother and always cherished? What right have you to do that?"

My stepmother didn't say a word; meanwhile, Milkot methodically removed a penknife from his pocket, went over to his wife, took the box from her hands, inserted his knife under its thin lid of Chinese varnish, and pried it open in a moment. The flimsy sides of the box broke, fragments clattered to the floor, and Michel's letters scattered all over the table. I threw myself at them and covered them with my body; Milkot seized me by the waist. Our struggle was brief – his strength was too great. He forced me away from the table and sat me down in a chair. Then he stood facing me and, arms crossed on his chest, stared at me fixedly. I was gasping from various powerful emotions and tried several times to stand up. Each time he took my arm and forced me back down in the chair.

"This is despicable," I said finally. "It's base coercion!"

"That's not the point," he replied coldly, with contempt. "Now tell me just who you think you are? How will you make amends to honest folk for the dishonor you've brought upon us? How will you repay us for the abuse that this morning was hurled at your stepmother, at your honest stepmother? Do you know what she's been subjected to, all because of you?"

"I don't know," I said, "and don't care to find out from you."

"Yes," said my stepmother, shoving Michel's letters into her handbag. "Madame Velina told me that your company corrupts young women and, having a grown daughter, she can no longer receive a person of such dubious conduct. Do you understand that? What do you have to say for yourself?"

"It's vulgar slander and doesn't deserve any reply," I said.

"Confess everything," said Milkot, taking me by the arm and making me stand up from the chair.

"Leave me alone," I said, managing to break away from him. "Leave me alone. Your treatment of me is intolerable and distressing."

"Is that so?" he said with irony. "If you please, you no longer have the right to present yourself as an innocent, oppressed victim; your pride is inappropriate. Be so good as to answer me at once and confess everything, do you hear? I don't know what's restraining me and why I don't give you what you really deserve."

"What do you want?" I asked. "What more can you do to me?"

I sat back down in the chair because my trembling legs refused to support me.

"Just look at her," said Milkot, turning to my stepmother and pointing at me. "Look! Instead of repentance, only indignation and impudence! No tears, not a word about forgiveness."

"Never!" I cried. "Weep? Beg forgiveness? Why? What for? Because you've tormented me since my childhood?"

"Do you know what you are?" he began again in a thunderous

voice. "You're merely a depraved woman, a disgrace to your family, the open mistress of a man you've thrust yourself upon. He was infatuated with you – that was obvious to everyone. You couldn't convince him to take you away from here; and if he didn't want to, it's only because men don't desire women who've nothing left to give. Every man wants to have an honest woman as his wife, not someone of such disgraceful conduct – that's suitable only in a mistress."

"My God! My God!" I cried, jumping up from the chair, wringing my hands in despair. "Father! Father! Where are you? Hear what they are saying to me!"

"Antonina," my stepmother objected heatedly. "How dare you call upon your father! You're profaning his good, honest name. He's fortunate not to have lived to see this disgrace. He'd never have withstood your dishonorable behavior and would have cursed you."

I fell silent, stunned by these words. But, after a moment's despair, turning to my stepmother, I suddenly recovered my strength, provoked by her undeserved and cruel words. I said to her more coldly than even I could expect after such a shock:

"Don't you ever use my father's name or defile his memory. Don't you call down his curses on anyone's head – he was incapable of such behavior. Even if I could imagine that terrible possibility in his soul, it would never have been directed at me – that much I know."

"My God!" retorted my stepmother. "This is terrible! This woman has nothing – no soul, no feeling – only rage! Be careful! Don't drive me to extremes! Don't wipe away the last traces of pity I feel – I won't stand for it! My just curses will fall upon your wicked head."

"That's up to you," I said. "I couldn't have done anything to deserve it; consequently, I'll endure it."

"Silence!" said Milkot in such a thunderous voice that I shuddered involuntarily. "Silence, or I'll destroy you! Enough! Now, hear my decision: you'll remain here until further notice. You have no right to cross this threshold, do you hear? Moreover, you will be locked in: that will be best! Let's go, Madame Milkot."

They left and locked the door. Can I possibly describe my despair? I still didn't understand how I'd become ensnared in this terrible net. I struggled desperately like Laocoön's children,* crushed by the mighty coils of monstrous serpents. There were no tears in my eyes; I suddenly recovered all my fading energy and rushed headlong into battle, without worrying whether it was ruin or rescue that awaited me. In hopeless despair, I resolved to act and to escape, no matter what, from the perpetual torment in which I was living.

Three weeks passed like this. Thousands of plans devised in the evening or at night dissolved during the day as I was confronted by forced inactivity and the complete impossibility of undertaking anything. My maid was dismissed and a new one was hired; I lived without any news of Michel and realized that someone had betrayed us again. But who? I didn't know and couldn't imagine. I wasn't allowed to go anywhere, not even into the drawing room. I was locked in my room and permitted to come out only for dinner. I wrote a letter to Michel and resolved to dispatch it at the first available opportunity.

One morning, Madame Beillant arrived to pay me one of her customary visits. They'd probably forgotten all about her and the maid let her into my room. My stepmother wasn't at home; I took advantage of the opportunity, told her everything, and begged her tearfully to deliver my letter. She wept upon hearing my story, consoled me as if I were her own daughter, but as soon as I asked her to take a letter to Michel B**, she looked sad and serious, and refused in no uncertain terms, saying that she didn't think she had any right to do it.

"Listen," I said to her. "Deliver this letter: I give you my word you're the only way I have to reach him. I've resolved to do anything. If you don't take it, I'll hand it to the first person I meet and won't spare myself. I won't stay locked in here forever. If I don't find someone who'll agree to deliver it, I'll escape and take it to him myself. Don't destroy me."

"Antonina, my child," she said. "You're not in your right mind. You don't recollect or realize what you're saying. You're terribly upset."

"Will you or won't you take this letter?" I asked decisively. "Remember, if you refuse, you're taking a great responsibility on yourself. My papa entrusted me to you, and now you don't want to help me."

"Your father wouldn't help you now and wouldn't want you to write."

"Why not?" I asked. "My love is innocent and their slander can't blacken it. I'm free, and so is Michel – where's the crime? I'm asking his assistance to find a final solution to our predicament – what's immoral about that?"

"His aunt hasn't given her consent," she replied softly.

"He can confirm that. I'll remain calm and take measures to escape my tyrants."

"Antonina," Madame Beillant said sternly. "Come to your senses. You're talking about your father's wife."

"About Mr. Milkot," I said, "who took control of her and has been tormenting me for a very long time," I added.

We both fell silent.

"Will you or won't you take my letter?" I asked insistently.

She looked into my eyes and, probably reading in them the resolution of despair, said timidly:

"Give it to me. I'll try to deliver it, but promise me you won't undertake anything without my advice and knowledge."

"All right," I said. "But I can't guarantee what I might do in a moment of despair."

She said a great deal more to me over a long time, trying to quiet me, and then left, promising to return. I waited for an answer, but none came. It was as if my letter, Michel, his family, and Vasily N** had all vanished into thin air. I was even more surprised because in this letter I'd asked Michel to deliver me from these incessant insults and to find me some refuge in or near Moscow where I could hide while Madame Beillant, acting on my behalf, persuaded my stepmother to allow me to take up a position elsewhere. I couldn't possibly live with them any longer. A week passed, then another began in perpetual and futile expectation. My relations with the Velins had been broken off completely; I didn't even hear Michel's name uttered. One evening my door opened exactly as it had a week and a half before; my stepmother and Milkot came in.

"So, you sent him another letter?" Milkot said with cold malice.

I was ready for anything and replied simply.

"I did."

"How?" he asked, gasping with rage.

I started laughing.

"I won't tell you," I replied.

"Is that so?" he said. "We'll see about that."

"You'll see," I replied calmly.

"Antonina, I want you to answer me: how did you manage to get a letter to him?" my stepmother asked peremptorily.

"I won't tell you," I replied. "Kill me if you like, but I won't. I'm not capable of such perfidy."

"We don't have to kill you," said Milkot. "Why such melodrama and a criminal act? That's unnecessary. But you can and should receive a beating."

"What?" I said, approaching my stepmother. "Will you allow him to beat me? Isn't it enough that he did that to me when I was a child? Doesn't he know there are laws against beating – if he doesn't recognize the law of conscience and honor?"

"Your conduct justifies such acts," my stepmother said coldly. "Promise me you won't have any further relations with Mr. B**, and we'll be more lenient with you."

"I can't make that promise, and I don't want to."

"What?" said Milkot, drawing near. "How dare you say that? I order you."

"Is that so?" I said sarcastically. "What rights have you over me? I'm not your daughter. Besides, if you wish, I will make a promise to you. I have written, I am writing, and I will continue to write – moreover, I'll escape this house at the first possible opportunity, I warn you. Those are my promises!"

I was in that insane state of tension where you don't recollect what you're saying or doing. My body was trembling; I felt a terrible chill in my veins and an unbearable physical pain in my heart.

"So, you're mocking us," said Milkot in a frenzied voice. He raised his hand and brought it down on me. "So there, now try mocking us!"

My stepmother threw herself between us, but it was too late. I reeled from the blow and fell into the chair; my cheek was burning, and I was in a terrible state of insanity, horror, and rage. She led her husband out of the room, forgetting to lock the door in her confusion, and accompanied him to his room. I stood up. Still reeling, I put on my hat, threw on a scarf and a jacket around my shoulders, and rushed out of my room. I ran quickly down the back staircase, opened the gate, raced along the street, turned the corner, and ran down the boulevard. In a quarter of an hour I rang the bell at Michel B**'s house. A servant opened the door.

"Is Mikhail Arkadich at home?" I asked.

He looked at me in astonishment and answered slowly:

"He is, ma'am. Who shall I say is calling?"

"No one. Is he alone or not?"

"He is, ma'am. No one's with him. He's in his own room," he replied.

"Tell him to come here; no, wait, take me to him."

The servant didn't know what to do. I put my hand in my pocket and took ten rubles from my purse, which I always had with me so as to be ready to escape at the earliest convenient moment.

"If you please," said the servant. "This way."

I went into the entry hall; the door led directly to Michel's rooms. There were two. I went into the first and saw him through the open door. He was sitting at his table writing a letter, his face bathed in tears. At that moment I saw everything, but could understand nothing.

"A lady to see you, sir, Mikhail Arkadich," said the servant, walking ahead of me. "Shall I ask her in? She's right here."

I stood behind him on the threshold of the second room.

"Who is it?" he asked without looking up.

"It's me, Michel," I said in French.

At the unexpected sound of my voice he started and quickly rose to meet me.

"Don't let anyone in," he said to his servant. "And don't say a word to anyone."

He followed the servant and, after seeing him out, locked the door.

"Did anyone see you come in here?" he asked me anxiously.

"No one, except for that man. And there may have been someone in the entry hall."

"My valet?"

"No."

"Well, thank heavens," he said, breathing more easily. "Tell me, what happened?"

"You must take me away at once," I said. "I can't stay in Milkot's house. It's reached the point now where they've started beating me."

"My God!" said Michel, falling to his knees before me. "My

God, what are they doing to us? What have we done to deserve such torment?"

I glanced at him coldly. I understood vaguely that he'd greeted me not as he should have, and that now I, the woman, instead of crying or protesting, was searching for a way out, while he, the man, was unable to find one and was asking why other people acted the way they did, and, like a child, blaming them for their hard-heartedness. But my coldness soon vanished at the sight of his tears, despair, timid caresses, and an embarrassment I could not understand. After we'd calmed down, as much as we could at such a difficult time, he said to me:

"Where will we go? Dmitry's not here, Vasily N** lives with his family, and they won't take you into a hotel without a passport or a permit."

"Haven't you found me an apartment yet?" I asked. "I wrote and asked you to. Did you receive my letter?"

"I did, but I couldn't look for one. You can't just take a young woman away from her family and conceal her against their will. Besides, just think, what would my relatives say? Judge for yourself."

He glanced at me; frightened by my gloomy expression as I listened to him, he added:

"I would have done it no matter what, but I thought you'd written in the first moment of rage after they confiscated my letters, and you hadn't quite decided what to do."

"When I decide something, my decision is always irrevocable," I said. "But we don't have time to discuss that now. I can't stay here. You must take me away."

"What about to Madame Beillant?" he said.

"I would have gone there myself if that had been possible. She lives in someone else's house; besides, they'll look for me there."

He became thoughtful.

"I don't know," he said. "I can't think of anything."

"If we pay enough at the hotel, they'll let me stay until tomorrow," I said. "By then you can find me a place to hide."

"Do you have any money?" he asked.

"Ten rubles."

"That's nothing. I have only twenty," he said. After a moment's thought, he added: "I'll send for Vasya N**. He'll come, bring some money, and give us advice. He'll think of something better; meanwhile, we can wait here."

He immediately scribbled a few lines on a scrap of paper, went into the entry hall, came back in to me, and locked the door behind him. He was suffering terrible anxiety; but, when he noticed that I was trembling all over, he gently covered me with the scarf that had slipped from my shoulders, wrapped my legs in his coat, and, after making me comfortable, sat down next to me and said:

"Now tell me in detail, if you can, what happened to you, my good, my poor Ninochka."

"First, tell me who betrayed us," I said.

"Betrayed?" he asked anxiously.

"Yes. I'd already written to say that the Velins knew everything and refused to receive my stepmother. But that's not all. Ten days ago I wrote again, and today my stepfather knew that. Tell me, explain what all this means. Did you tell anyone I wrote to you?"

He turned red.

"Yes," he said. "I told one of my women friends, but she . . . "

"Who?" I asked, cutting him off.

"I can vouch for her!"

"Who was it?" I repeated with force.

He was silent.

"Are you keeping secrets from me?"

"No, no! It was Katenka Velina."

"Katenka," I said. "Now I understand everything."

"I can vouch for her," he said again.

It was my turn to fall silent. A terrible suspicion entered my mind. There seemed to be a general conspiracy against me. His aunt, with her persecution, illness, and affection; Katenka, with her feigned friendship; and her family, with its obvious contempt, were all trying to extinguish his love for me. I sat there, my head lowered and resting on my hands. Several times he tried to pull my hands away from my face, which was distorted by conflicting feelings; failing to do so, he began speaking, at first softly, then with animation:

"Listen, Antonina," he said. "Don't blame me. I was in a terrible position. My aunt fell ill from grief when she found out that I wanted to marry you in secret. It's a horrible thing to be the cause of illness in the woman who was like a mother to me! My father reproached me for it – he wept often, sitting at her bedside, and his tears fell on my heart and burned right through it. When I entered my ailing aunt's room, she crowned my torment with her affectionate kindness. She forgave me everything; but other members of the household regarded me as if I were carrying the plague and kept their distance from me. Their silence and sad, depressed appearance were worse than a reproach. When I asked if my aunt was feeling better, they barely replied, as if they were surprised that I, the person who was killing her, could inquire and be concerned about her. I couldn't have endured all this if Katenka hadn't appeared on the scene as an angel of peace. She entreated my father to forgive me, reconciled my sisters with me, looked after my sick aunt, and made excuses for me in the eyes of everyone; she alone sympathized with my predicament. She felt sorry for me and even for you, although she honestly confessed that she'd never had any great affection for you. Nevertheless, she commiserated in our predicament, and her tender friendship consoled me more than once."

"Oh, I know," I cried, "how very clever she is."

"And kind," he said affirmatively. "In childhood you and she didn't get along, and that's left its traces on you both. You aren't fair to each other; if you recognized each other's worth and realized what kind, splendid hearts you both have, you'd be reconciled."

I glanced at him. He spoke simply, although heatedly.

"Tell me more," I said. "Did you show her my letters?"

"No. I merely told her about them and summarized their content."

"And she betrayed us."

"No, not her, no! Never! She knows I could never forgive her for doing that. She's honest and very attached to me."

"Attached," I repeated inanely.

"By friendship," he said indecisively and fell silent.

I had nothing further to say; my eyes wandered aimlessly and suddenly fell upon the paper lying on the table. It was the letter he was writing when I entered the room. I happened to notice my name at the top of the page and picked it up. He rushed over to me and ripped it from my hands.

"Was this letter addressed to me?" I asked.

"Of course," he replied. "You saw that yourself."

"Then don't I have the right to read it?"

"There's nothing to read, my dear. I've told you almost everything. If there's anything else to be conveyed, I'll come tell you myself; after all, you want to live apart, alone. Why hasn't Vasya come?" he added, after a pause. "He should be here by now; it's getting late."

He couldn't hide his obvious anxiety from me. Offended by his agitation and fear, I said:

"Don't worry, if he doesn't come within half an hour, I'll leave."

"I won't allow that," he replied heatedly. "What do you take me for? Anything can happen. We can part and be separated forever;

but to allow you to leave here alone, to deliver you into the hands of your family after your escape, to betray you in that way – that I cannot and will not do. Only a man lacking all honor and conscience would be capable of an act like that."

"I can take care of myself," I said. "You are losing all your rights over me, more and more every minute . . . "

"Why?" he asked, interrupting me nervously, and then suddenly falling silent as if struck by an unexpected thought.

At that very moment a loud knock at the door resounded so suddenly that it made us both shudder. Michel's expression changed and he turned terribly pale.

"Who's there?" he asked.

"It's me," a resolute voice replied.

He stood there like a lost soul and then went to the door.

"Auntie," he said, "I can't let you in. I've already undressed and gone to bed."

At the mention of his aunt's name, not a single drop of blood was left in my veins: all of it rushed to my heart and I was stifled by its rapid pounding.

"Open up at once," the voice continued. "I want to come in. If you don't let me in now, I'll send for your father. He'll have the door broken down, and that will be worse. Don't make a scandal. Open up, I command you."

"I can't," said Michel.

"Then I'll send for your father at once and for her stepmother. We'll see whether your willpower can withstand the assertion of our joint rights."

Michel turned the key in the lock. I glanced around quickly, but there was no place to hide. Moreover, I did that instinctively; I knew that I was lost and therefore I remained sitting motionless in the armchair.

"So, they didn't deceive me," Madame B** said upon entering the room, assuming a tragic pose and addressing only her nephew. "So, it's true. This is how you dare disgrace my house. With no regard for your innocent sisters you receive your lover only two steps away from them!"

I jumped up from my place.

"At least forbid her from speaking to me. I know that such women respect no limits and their insolence exceeds all bounds; insulting an honest woman, an irreproachable head of a household, merely affords them enjoyment and pleasure. I hope, however, that you still retain some feeling of nobility and will spare the woman who raised you, who has been a second mother to you. You won't allow her to be abused by a shameless woman."

I approached the sofa, picked up my hat, and hurriedly put it on.

"Antonina," said Michel, rushing up to me and blocking my way. "Where are you going? You're all alone. You can't go anywhere alone at night. Come with me. I'll escort you."

His aunt seized his arm.

"So, you want your behavior to be the death of me? I was close to death once – now you want to drive me to the grave – that's the thanks I get for taking care of you. My God! What have I done to deserve this punishment?" she said, crossing her arms and raising her eyes to the ceiling.

"Auntie," said Michel, throwing himself to his knees in front of her. "Mamenka,* be kind. I'll be right back. Just think, where can this young woman go? How can she leave here alone, at night? . . . "

"She can go the same way she came," she replied dryly and with contempt.

I was already at the door. Michel rushed after me and held me back by force.

"I will leave you," said his aunt, looking at him with indescribable rage. "I came to ask you not to dishonor my house. You have remained deaf to the voice of duty and morality. I'm going to fetch your father. He'll know how to get rid of this woman whose foot should never have crossed the threshold of an honest house, our family threshold, a woman who came here shamelessly to destroy the peace and happiness of our household and who pursues her lover on the very eve of his engagement." DAMN

I turned around.

"Engagement," I said horrified, not believing what I heard.

"No, not yet, Antonina!" Michel cried in a voice that rent the soul.

"You're an actress, madam," she said, looking at me with contempt. "Did you really not know what the whole town already does? Madame Velina took the trouble to inform your stepmother about the engagement of her daughter to my nephew. Consequently, you . . . "

I don't remember what she said next – I didn't hear another word. My eyes looked wildly at the two of them, at his aunt's triumphant, radiant expression, and at Michel's pale, distorted face. He was still holding my hand. I pulled myself away from him forcefully, tore my hand free, and rushed out of the room. On the threshold I came face to face with Vasily N**.

"Take me away from here! Quickly, quickly!"

"My God, what's wrong?" he asked, taking my hand.

Muffled sobs and someone's tight grasp on the folds of my dress forced me to turn around. Michel knelt before me, his head bowed; I could barely make out the words in the sounds produced by his heartrending voice:

"Antonina! Forgive me."

I stopped and straightened up. I both pitied and despised him at that moment. Freeing my dress from his convulsive grasp, I said distinctly and resolutely:

"I wish you happiness – and, I forgive you."

Without hesitating another moment, I left the room. Vasily N** sat me in his carriage and asked where to take me.

"Wherever you like," I replied. "It's all the same."

Later I was told that when we arrived and I had to get out of the carriage, Vasily found me unconscious and carried me up to my room.

When I came to, I saw the good Madame Beillant sitting at my bedside. I opened my weak eyes and gradually began looking around the room, as if I wanted to remember something, but I couldn't endure the strain and closed my eyes again. I felt exhausted; my entire body ached and I lacked the strength to sit up or even to change my position. In a little while I opened my eyes again and glanced around; the table had been moved next to the bed and was covered with medicines. In general, my room looked different. A strange disorder prevailed: my books, portraits, and music were all gathered up in one pile; linens were strewn everywhere; there were mustard plasters and various other accoutrements of a sickroom. Madame Beillant sat there silently doing some handiwork; at times she glanced up at me and then returned to her work. I felt great pain in my head and, raising my hand, pressed my temple and felt something cold. Madame Beillant stood up and adjusted the cold compress on my head. I uttered her name in a weak voice; she merely looked at me, said nothing in reply, and continued sitting there motionless. I called her again. She stood up.

"What happened to me?" I asked.

"Nothing much. You fell ill, but now, thank God, you're better," she said with joy.

"My head hurts – a great deal; it really aches."

"Be patient, my dear, the doctor will be here soon."

I was very weak and so I closed my eyes again and lay there without thinking, almost asleep, resting. Soon another voice summoned me from this state of oblivion.

"Well now? How is she?" it said.

"Better. She just came to and spoke with me calmly, complaining of a headache."

"Yes, doctor," I said, "my head hurts."

"Take the ice away. It's no longer needed," said the doctor. "Everything's all right; her pulse is weak but steady."

"How long have I been ill?" I asked.

"Don't talk now, don't say anything," the doctor replied.

He prescribed some medicine and went away, asking that I be left in peace. I fell asleep and woke up feeling better and fresher.

"How long have I been ill?" I asked Madame Beillant.

"Three weeks, dear."

I started thinking; I tried to recall everything that had happened. I rubbed my forehead but couldn't remember anything. I had nothing to compare my present condition to; I was like someone who wakes up trying to recall a dream that's completely vanished from his memory. For several days I was so weak that all my efforts to reconstruct the past resulted in my falling asleep. When I felt better and could think again – my memory returned by chance and suddenly shed bright light on my oblivion. Once the maid came into my room and, sorting linens in my wardrobe, took out some of my things, including my kerchief and hat. At the sight of them I cried out, seized hold of my head, and sat up in bed.

"Antonina, Antonina!" Madame Beillant cried involuntarily. "What's wrong, my dear?"

"Is he getting married?" I asked. "Yes, he is! It wasn't a dream. He's getting married!"

"Calm down, my dear. Don't think about a thing."

Physical illness is beneficial, my friends, physical weakness is beneficial for a broken heart. It deadens the moral suffering by consuming a person's strength; she's too weak even for inner torment. After this new shock that I couldn't bear, I felt faint; then exhaustion and weakness overcame me again, and I passed the days in uninterrupted sleep. I recovered slowly; only when I could get out of bed did I learn that I had been suffering from inflammation of the brain and had hovered between life and death for two weeks. And now, by the will of fate, I was restored to existence once again, but was unable to resume my life immediately. Madame Beillant told me that my stepmother had been very moved by my illness, had even wept, and more than once had tried to look after me. But I wouldn't let her get near me and, recognizing her even in my unconscious state, I became so agitated that the doctor forbade her to sit with me. That troubled and saddened her even more.

"Do you really not want to see her?" Madame Beillant asked. "Your illness has grieved her greatly. You should make your peace with her."

"If she wishes to see me, I'm ready. Ask her to come," I said with a deep sigh.

I won't relate in detail the first meeting with my stepmother, during which we silently took each other's hand and exchanged not a single word about the past, nor will I describe my initial reflections after the meeting. I merely regretted that I hadn't died and was no longer concerned with any of this. Madame Beillant came every day and chatted with me, avoiding any subject that might provoke the painful emotion of the past; she read to me, and, when I began to go out, came to fetch me in a carriage and took me out for rides.

It was the beginning of April. The sun was shining brightly, streams of water were coursing noisily through the streets, and the invigorating spring air was penetrating my breast bracingly. I shall never forget the painful impression I experienced on the first day's outing when the playful rays of the sun suddenly penetrated the open window of the carriage and flashed into my eyes, lighting everything with a bright radiance. Sunlight played on rooftops and sparkled on the crosses and gilded cupolas of churches; it shone on banks of snow piled high on both sides of the road, slippery stones, and walls of houses. Carriages rumbled down the bare pavement, coaches rushed by with smiling, well-dressed ladies, pedestrians forged ahead cheerfully. I was struck by the festive appearance that the onset of spring imparted, particularly to the city, noisily filling its previously deserted streets with people. It made me vividly aware that being alive was good, cheerful, and joyous for everyone but me. This animated picture of other people's lives, under the clear radiance of the sun, amid the rebirth of nature, made me take a good look at myself, and I was horrified by the emptiness, silence, and deathly chill in my heart. Seeing the sun was particularly difficult and disturbing. Somehow it cast its light on my exhausted figure joyfully and peeped cheerfully into my lifeless eyes, and, when it appeared, they filled with uninvited tears. I quietly lowered the shade and asked to return home.

When I got out of the carriage and laboriously returned to my room feeling tired and worn out, copious but involuntary tears eased the constriction in my heart. I pitied no one, wept for nothing, but felt pained and distressed: I wanted to die.

The next day I said to Madame Bcillant:

"Listen, I have a favor to ask you."

"What may I do for you?"

"Is it possible to locate Dmitry Z**? He must have returned from Petersburg."

"He's back in Moscow. He came often to ask after you during your illness."

"I want to see him."

"That's very easy to arrange, but not right now; any shock might do you harm."

"There won't be any," I said. "Now I can feel neither grief nor shock."

"Well, all right, I'll bring him to you."

And indeed, a few days later, Dmitry came to see me. Our meeting was very strange. He was staggered by my altered face and tried to say something, but his voice betrayed him: he kissed my hand in silence. On the other hand, I felt or appeared completely at ease and chatted with him so dispassionately that even I was surprised. I asked him to tell me everything he knew. At first he resisted, but then, seeing my persistence, fulfilled my request. Although he tried to spare my former feelings for Michel and didn't want to cause me pain, I noticed from what he said that, although he pitied his friend, he felt total contempt for the weakness of character that had led him to agree to marry a woman he didn't love. Dmitry didn't know Katenka Velina very well and therefore couldn't judge her; nevertheless, her conduct seemed not altogether innocent; Michel, of course, blamed Vasily N** for revealing our correspondence, and his sister even more; but Dmitry and I were convinced that it wasn't true; we knew that we owed our misfortunes to Katya and her mother, who so skillfully managed to befriend the members of Michel B***'s household, work together as mediators of their family affairs, and achieve their desired goal. Michel's agreement to marry Katya on the very day of my insane intrusion was being pressed on him but was not yet final; at least, that's what he assured Dmitry. Whatever the case, his marriage was celebrated the first Sunday after Easter. Dmitry told me that Michel looked gloomy and in general showed traces of extreme depression, while Katya tried to please both him and his family; he was amicably affectionate to her, nothing more.

"My fate is so strange," I said. "It seems I could still rejoice in his happiness with her; but, since I won't get to see him, I'm deprived even of that consolation. I've known her since childhood. She seeks power, and he's weak. She'll control him: then what will happen?"

"He'll pass from his aunt's hands into his wife's. He was born to live under someone's eternal protection," said Dmitry.

"He won't be happy," I said.

"Perhaps not," he replied.

"It's horrible! So horrible!" I said, starting to cry.

"What's so horrible about it?" he retorted. "Let him experience what suffering's all about. I'll be pleased. If I feel sorry for anyone, it certainly won't be for him." *Porry*

"Dmitry! Dmitry!" I said.

"Forgive me, my dear Antonina, but I can't love him any longer. I always knew he was weak, but I never thought he'd sink to such childish impotence. I don't respect such people."

"Silence," I said. "That hurts me; let's never speak of it again. All that is dead and buried in both me and you – isn't that so?"

"Yes," he said. "But we'll remain friends, won't we?"

I gave him my hand as a sign of agreement. We were both silent.

"One more question," I said. "The last one. When I was ill, did he send to ask about me?"

"Not here, but to me. He couldn't do otherwise – that is, he didn't dare."

I smiled sadly; Dmitry left soon afterward. We parted friends.

When I had completely recovered, I asked Madame Beillant to find me a position without fail. I had discussed it with my stepmother, and made her understand that I could not consent to live in the same house with Milkot and sought permission to leave them. My stepmother consented to everything I wanted; she merely requested, through Madame Beillant, that I make my peace with Milkot. But I couldn't and didn't want to hear anything about him. In spite of everyone's entreaties, I left the house without seeing him.

I took a position in the home of Baroness Minskaya and carried out my obligations in a completely automatic way. Her two girls were my pupils. At first their mother was present for all my lessons; but then, either because she had gained complete confidence in me or because she had done as much as form demanded, she stopped visiting our classroom and left her children entirely to me. The baroness was cold, refined, and proud – an exemplary wife and mother, as her acquaintances used to say. When I arrived in her home, she explained my duties and her expectations; from what she said I concluded that the maintenance of strict propriety was her principal demand. Since my health was still very bad, I reserved several hours a day for myself and used the time to rest from the lessons. In general, everything tired me out, and I sank into extreme apathy, a state that erased any moral needs of my own. I got up at the appointed hour, gave my lessons, got dressed for dinner, and then, immediately afterward, retired to my room, where I sat doing nothing. In the evening everyone gathered in the parlor for tea: the whole family sat sedately around the table and dispersed after an hour or so of insignificant conversation. The baron left for his club, the baroness went visiting, and I withdrew upstairs with the children, where they prepared their lessons. At nine o'clock I escorted them to their bedroom adjoining mine and heard their evening prayers. After getting them into bed, I retreated to my room and spent most of my evenings alone, doing almost nothing, in a state of benumbed tranquillity. Sometimes I was as depressed as if a lead weight were pressing on my bosom. I felt like crying and wanted to shed tears, but couldn't summon them from the depths of my soul; it was as if they'd frozen in my bosom, as if their source had dried up in the deadly cold that so burdened me. Sometimes I remembered my entire past and felt pity for myself, weeping over my sad fate; but these attempts were futile. Insensibility and stupefaction gripped me. When July came we moved to the dacha. Warm summer air, greenery, fields, and strolls all revived me somewhat. My health improved, but I had yet to recover my lost vitality; everything had been crushed. I existed mechanically, most likely because I lacked the strength to think about anything, even whether I would be better off ending the joyless, aimless existence I was leading. I accepted the customs of the household with indifference; I hardly noticed the baroness's cool treatment; if she happened to make some remarks to me in her gentle but imposing way, I heard her out and did exactly as she asked, without reflection or coercion. It was all the same to me where or how I went on living; my indifference to everything and everybody had reached an extreme.

Madame Beillant visited me every Sunday and questioned me with concern. Was I all right? Was I content? I answered in the affirmative; as a matter of fact, it was all the same to me, good or bad; I'd lost all my previous inclinations and had no desires whatever. I had loved music and always used to play; now I never even opened the piano, and, although I gave lessons to my two pupils, never played. Formerly, I liked getting dressed up; now I wore the dresses my maid handed to me. I didn't read anything. Summer passed, and when autumn came we returned to Moscow. I didn't think about Michel much and even deliberately avoided saying his name. It now seemed to me that I didn't love him at all – as if I'd forgotten that I'd ever known him and loved him. Soon, however, I had to acknowledge that that was simply the delusion of a tormented heart. I realized that my heart still retained some sort of incomprehensible feeling for him, if not love, then traces of sympathy and attachment. Winter was nearing its end; it flew by for me unnoticed, monotonously and painfully, in the boundless wasteland where I lived, leaving me at the mercy of others and retreating, as it were, from myself. The baron had the habit of telling his wife at tea and dinner all the news he heard the previous evening at the club. One day at teatime when I was present as usual, sitting there mechanically, I was suddenly roused from my deep slumber by the sound of Michel B"'s name uttered by the baron in his deep bass voice. With a shudder I began paying attention to his conversation with his wife.

"Really?" said the baroness. "The poor wife!"

"She doesn't know it, nor does his aunt."

"Can't they see? If he disappears from home for days at a time, surely they must know where he is?"

The baron started laughing.

"That's a fine thing!" he said. "How would you discover where I was? If I wanted to waste my fortune on actresses, how would you stop me?"

"That's an entirely different matter," the baroness retorted. "You're well on in years, while Michel B** is still just a lad."

"Well, I swear he's carousing like a grown man; he drinks for nights at a time. Yesterday he presented Mademoiselle Henriette with a brooch worth four thousand rubles; he always acts as her partner when she plays faro.* And you know, you've probably heard that she's a dreadful gambler. His wealth won't last long if she's the one looking after it and she stays his mistress a little while longer."

"Shh . . . " the baroness said suddenly, pointing at the children. "How many times have I asked you to be more discreet about what you say – what expressions you use!"

"Well, my dear, enough of that. One can't always be so cautious – it's a deadly bore!"

"Mademoiselle Stein," said the baroness, turning to me. "It's time for the children to go upstairs."

I stood up and led them away. They soon went to bed; I returned to my room and a striking transformation took place within me – that name, that news, produced in me a long-forgotten painful agitation. I burst into tears and, resting my head on my arms, sat for a long time weeping over his pitiful lot. Yes, I felt sorry for him; this emotion awoke forcefully in me and, undiluted by any other feeling, filled my soul. Michel, that tender, timid, quiet man, was drinking night after night, gambling with actresses, spending his nights in orgies – that must mean he was terribly unhappy. That bitter certainty suddenly compelled me to forgive him for the past; compassion and friendship flooded my heart. The next day I sent for Dmitry Z**, who came at once. Since I'd been living with the baroness, I saw him infrequently and had never once mentioned Michel's name in conversation; he too never referred to him. Now, after admitting Dmitry, I asked him as soon as he came into my room:

"What is Michel B** up to?"

"He's destroying himself," he replied coldly.

"My God!" I said. "Is it really impossible to save him?"

"I don't know," he replied. "But, after all, is he worth the effort? Does he deserve pity? This may astonish you – but what is he to you? Leave it alone and forget him."

"I had forgotten all about him as long as I imagined him happy and content; but to know that he's suffering – that he could fling himself into such a life from torment alone . . . "

"Who knows whether it's belated regrets or pangs of conscience – perhaps he's haunted by your image as well."

"What? Me?" I said. "Could I be the cause of his new misfortunes? Don't say that. My God, as if this weren't enough! I have neither the strength nor the will to face it!"

I burst into tears.

"Listen," I said. "You love me. Go to him."

"I've stopped seeing him," he replied tranquilly.

"Why? What for? He loved you so much."

"I no longer love him."

"Silence! Silence!" I said forcefully. "If you love me at least a little, you must go to him. Tell him I'm completely content with my fate; I ask him not to grieve over me, and the main thing, I ask him in the name of our past love to change his way of life. It will destroy his good name, his health, his heart. Won't you do this?" I asked him. "In that case, I'll write him a letter; that will be terribly difficult for me. Please spare me that torment."

Dmitry promised to call on him and convey my message. During the ensuing days I was overcome with anxiety; my desire to know what he was doing was so powerful that I recovered my previous energy and, wanting to show Michel that I harbored no regrets and was no longer suffering, I accompanied Madame Beillant on a series of visits to all her acquaintances and was invited to several parties in the French colony.* Madame Beillant was acquainted with many merchants and, taking advantage of my momentary desire, she made haste to introduce me to many people she knew. For five months I heard nothing about Michel – he'd vanished from the social sphere. Dmitry told me that my plea had caused that change in his behavior, turning him back to family life. When he found out that I was at peace and going out often in society, he was somewhat reconciled with his own past. If he was still suffering from our separation, it was more in relation to himself than to me, since he was convinced that I'd totally forgotten him and no longer cared for him.

Once I had agreed to accompany Madame Beillant, I couldn't refuse to visit our mutual friends during the holidays; finding diversion in society, I didn't want to deprive myself of the melancholy relief of forgetting my own sadness. Gradually I began to emerge from that frozen state in which I'd languished for more than two years after the blow that had struck me so unexpectedly and forcefully. I awoke from moral death – I was young and my youth proclaimed itself: it got its own way and continued its appointed task, resurrecting me little by little. Youth alone refreshed my tormented, lacerated heart with its vital force; it healed my wounds. And if a dull ache erupted from time to time, still I had come back to life and could bear it.

We often visited the wife of a French banker with whose family Madame Beillant was on very good terms. I became close friends with them and found great enjoyment in their pleasant, small circle made up of well-educated, broadly experienced people. They were almost all foreigners. Once I was introduced to a Mr. Bertini, an

Italian, recently arrived, a young man of about thirty-five, tall and swarthy, resembling a Creole. His face struck me – it was remarkable and extremely expressive. He was a wealthy Florentine merchant who'd come to establish a trading house in Moscow and planned to settle down in Russia for some time to oversee the progress of his affairs. He was very intelligent and well-educated – his first words drew us together. It seemed that he knew all my father's relatives and was on good terms with his younger brother. I didn't pay Bertini any particular attention, however; there was nothing special between us except for a simple expression of friendship, since he was in close contact with my uncle. I chatted with him frequently about them; he provided many details about the whole Stein family of Mainz. Our evenings were devoted to such conversations. Three months had passed since we had first become acquainted and it was now summertime. The baroness was not feeling very well, and her doctor had advised her to drink the waters at some Moscow mineral springs. I was prescribed the same; she proposed that I accompany her every morning. We began our course of treatment in early June; we set off for Ostozhenka* every morning at eight o'clock. When he heard that I was also there for the treatment, Bertini showed up at the springs every morning, assuring me that he, too, was taking the waters; while the baroness strolled with her acquaintances, he would spend all his time with me, never leaving my side even for a moment. He had seen a great deal, traveled widely, and knew how to convey his impressions eloquently. My acquaintanceship with him, bolstered by these daily meetings and strolls, soon became a close personal friendship. His company did me good – he distracted me. We talked about everything, most of all the southern countries I'd long dreamed of visiting. He described in brilliant colors the charming beauty of nature, the fascination of a different way of life, and the enjoyment afforded by great works of art. Bertini was direct in his speech and ardent even in his stories.

Toward the end of the summer, I don't know how it happened, but he fell in love with me, passionately in love. As soon as I realized it, all the enjoyment I found in his company disappeared. I began to avoid him. He was so staggered by this change in the way I treated him that he became morose, but still pursued me relentlessly, and rapidly switched from extreme tenderness and a desire to please to adamant, sometimes insolent indiscretions, for which he'd immediately repent and ask my forgiveness. Once he offered me his arm, inviting me for a stroll in the garden; I wanted to refuse, but, after glancing at his face, dared not say a word. I gave him my arm in silence and we set off.

"Tomorrow you finish taking the waters?" he asked.

"Yes," I said. "Our course of treatment has ended."

"That, it seems, is my sentence – I'll have no chance to see you anymore."

"Oh, no! Sundays I shall be visiting Madame T**."

"Once a week," he said. "So little!"

"What's to be done?" I replied mechanically, thinking about something else.

"Mademoiselle Stein," he said suddenly, his voice trembling. "I love you, you know that. Yes, you do, because you've begun avoiding me, as if you were afraid of me, afraid of my love. Don't you love me?"

"Oh, no!" I said. "I love you very much, but only as a friend."

"That's not enough for me," he said, continuing with the ardor and passion of an Italian. "No! No! You must grow to love me. Is it possible that my passion has yet to find a way into your childlike heart, to melt it, to set it on fire? That's impossible! Listen to me – I've never loved anyone like this. Allow me to love you; I'm sure the fire that burns in my heart will also kindle yours."

"I'm unable to love," I said sadly.

He looked at me, grew pale, and asked apprehensively:

"Really? Do you love someone else?"

"I did love someone else, but I don't any longer," I replied. "My heart is dead to love."

"Don't believe that! Don't – it's deception. At your age your heart could not have grown cold and rejected life's greatest blessing forever! I'm sure it will live again – my passion will fan the spark and when you realize how ardently I love you, you'll come to share my feeling."

I was silent.

"I will hope," he said.

His hand trembled, his eyes shone; glancing at him, I was instinctively afraid of the passionate gaze he directed at me.

"Later," I said timidly. "I'm still ill. You've caught me unawares. I'm confused and can't give you an answer now."

We returned to the gallery. The baroness was waiting for me and we left at once. The next morning Madame Beillant came to see me.

"I've come on an errand," she said. "Bertini seeks your hand and wants your final answer."

"I can't marry," I replied.

"But he told me you didn't refuse him once and for all."

"I felt sorry for him. He was so deeply affected."

"Listen, Antonina, don't ruin your life. You'll regret it later. Just think. You have no one at all: no family, no friends, no fortune."

"What of it? My present position is my fortune, and I do have some friends – don't you care for me?"

"A dependent position is very difficult, my child; the older you get, the more painful it will become for you. Your life wilted at its first flowering. Won't you allow yourself to be revived? Bertini loves you with a mad love that's rarely encountered; believe me, the happiness of being loved is not the last and hardly the best part of married love. He's rich – he'll pamper you and seek to please you. You'll love him as a friend. You'll have a family, children. Do you really want to reject all this, to turn away from these blessings? Why? What for?"

I didn't know what to say, but I couldn't agree with her and kept silent.

"Think. Don't refuse him. If you only knew how he loves you, if you could see him today, you'd take pity on him."

"But I don't love him. I'll never be able to love anyone," I said.

"So what? Let him love you, and you'll come to love him later, out of gratitude. I'm certain of that. He's a clever man, honest, and very wealthy. You know that all the mothers are eager to snare him for their daughters; not one banker's daughter, no matter how rich, would ever refuse him."

"What do I care about that?" I said sadly.

Madame Beillant, seeing that my vanity was silent, went on at length about family happiness and a quiet life. I'd never known such a life and was involuntarily charmed by the picture she painted. Still, I didn't give my consent; Madame Beillant left without any final answer. On Sunday I found Bertini at Madame T***'s. When he saw me, his expression changed; as I was leaving, he asked permission to come and visit me. I hesitated.

"It will be our last meeting," he said abruptly.

I agreed. He appeared the next day, his face showing all the signs of a terrible spiritual agitation.

"Decide my fate," he said, growing pale.

I tried to speak, but he seized my hand.

"Silence!" he said. "Silence! First hear me out. You must know what you mean to me. I love you; I adore you. I am overwhelmingly attracted to everything about you: your pallor, your blond curls, and your dark eyes that remind me of my distant homeland and its wonderful women. But you're much lovelier than they are. Your face is full of pensive charm, your figure is as airy as a fairy tale. I adore you. Your slightest wish will be my command. I shall leave and take you away from here; I will give up everything to amuse and comfort you. You love nature – I'll take you to where it has flowered abundantly. You love the arts – I'll procure all their pleasures for you. Money will become important to me only inasmuch as it can satisfy your desires, whims, and tastes! I'll sit at your feet – my whole life will be devoted to pleasing you forever. Don't refuse me, don't reject my love – my ardent love!"

He threw himself at me and seized my hand, clinging to it passionately and fervently. I burst into tears.

"I value your love," I said. "I believe in it; I thank you for it with all the fullness of my heart. But how can I ever repay you? You don't know to whom you're giving your heart and your love so generously. They deserve great recompense – I'm not worthy of them."

"What does that mean?" he asked, his voice trembling.

"I've told you already that I loved someone else and buried my heart in that love."

"But that's all passed – you – you no longer love him?"

"I don't," I said.

"So why talk about something that doesn't exist? I implore you: don't torment me, don't torture me by describing what could have been mine, but which I don't have. I came too late; I curse myself for my tardy arrival, but how could I have known, how could I have foreseen, that in this cold, faraway Russia I'd find the dream of my life?"

He looked at me, devouring me with his eyes. After noticing his gaze, I lowered my head and was silent, overwhelmed with conflicting emotions.

What can I tell you, my friends? I stood my ground that time, too, and did not give my consent. But he pursued me with love, entreaties, and treats. My slightest desire was divined; he learned my tastes and tried to gratify them as best he could. Once, when I arrived home, I found that in my absence my entire room had been enchantingly decorated with flowers. For the new year's holiday he sent me flowers and candy again. I was his sole concern; at long last one final attention touched me more deeply than all words or compliments. I knew a poor family that could hardly eke out an existence, and I used to help them as much as I could. One day I dropped in on them and was astonished by the prosperity in which they were living: their room had been furnished with everything they needed; the husband had a job with a decent salary; the wife, her old mother, and the children were all well-clothed. They surrounded me with such tears of gratitude, with the joy of poor people whose life has been magically transformed from anguish to happiness. I began to weep with them, but I couldn't convince them that I was not the cause of their good fortune, not their savior, as they called me.

I had barely returned home when Bertini came to see me. I began to thank him, but I couldn't go on; I sat down on a chair and, under the influence of my impressions, again began to cry. He took advantage of my deeply moved state and once more launched his assault.

"Don't destroy me," he said in conclusion. "Agree to serve as my guide, a protector of the poor and suffering – you'll be their guardian angel. This is our last meeting. I swear to you, if I leave here without hope, I shall throw myself into a reckless life, destroying both my heart and my passion. If I don't succeed, I'll finish myself off with a pistol and a bullet. I can no longer live between fear and hope, between the thirst for bliss and the terror of loneliness. Have you yet to fall in love with me? Is your heart really so implacable and frigid, like the ice floes of your second homeland?"

/ "If your happiness can only be found in me," I said with trepidation, extending my hand to him, "then take it. I give my consent, but on one condition." \

His ecstasy knew no bounds and he looked insane; he didn't hear anything further. Falling to my feet, he kissed them with such fervent and chaotic exaltation that I felt apprehensive. I got up and moved away from him.

"You're forgetting the condition," I said.

My cheeks were flushed with shame and a terrible, incomprehensible emotion in which confusion, timidity, and involuntary alienation contended. I almost regretted giving my consent.

"Your conditions are my commandments," he said. "I'm prepared to do anything."

"You're to come again tomorrow and hear a full confession of my past," I said. "And then, if you still want me, I'll agree to become your wife." ⏐ Why tho

"I don't want to know anything. I don't want to hear anything," he said. "Why such torment at the best moment of my life? I remember only your last word. It's wonderful! Intoxicating!"

"Bertini," I said in earnest. "I want you to know my past. I don't want to have any secrets from you. Without that I can't agree to unite my fate with yours."

"As you wish," he said. "I'll be here tomorrow."

The next day I told him in detail the story of my love. It made a terrible impression on his passionate temperament. He blushed, paled, and when I finished, he said to me:

"I have endured the torments of hell! You'll never love me as you loved him."

I tried to say something . . .

"I know, I know," he said, interrupting me. "Be still, don't deliver that blow. You loved him, but you will only tolerate me."

"No," I said. "I value your heart and your love, and I love you with tender friendship."

He took hold of his head.

"Your friendship isn't enough – I almost despise it. But you'll come to love me, yes, you will. I want that to happen and it will! I'll live for you alone and through you. As for now, let me go. I don't know what I'm saying or doing. Good-bye."

He left without even taking the hand I extended to him. The unbridled nature of his emotions frightened me. The next day he came to see me again. He was morose and gloomy.

"Antonina," he said to me. "I, too, must tell you something. . . . You see, this bit of news may . . . perhaps be unpleasant for you to hear. But let me assure you beforehand that it won't affect our life together in any way. Up to now I couldn't decide whether to tell you. I have a daughter . . . " чит

I'd known that he was a widower, but had never heard anything about a daughter.

"Where is she?" I asked.

"It's unpleasant to become a stepmother at your age, and of course it would be difficult for you to take on the responsibilities of motherhood. But you don't have to worry. Without going into unnecessary, painful details, I can only say that I was unhappy with my wife and feel no love for my daughter. I decided to raise her far away and entrusted her to my aunt in Florence. But my aunt died, and three months ago an Italian family visiting Russia agreed to bring her here. She's here in a boarding school, and there she will stay. I'm fulfilling my obligation, but I can't love her – nor should I."

"What are you saying?" I asked. "Can it be possible not to love a daughter?"

"Don't blame me. Believe what I say. I can't love her. Why not? I can't tell you, but I have my reasons."

"Does she have bad tendencies?" I asked.

"No, I don't think so. But I don't know. I rarely see her."

"I want to meet her," I said.

"Why?"

"I definitely want to meet her. I beg you, bring her to see me."

At first he wouldn't agree to my request, but finally, in view of my persistence, he yielded to my desire. Lenochka's appearance aroused in me both pity and deep sympathy for her. You know her already – at that time she was still wild and taciturn, but her face was expressive and suggested that she would be quick to form attachments; besides, she reminded me of my own situation and how my stepmother had behaved toward me, and I resolved to become her mother. My insistence forced her father to promise to bring his daughter into our household right after our wedding. Soon afterward, my engagement was announced. My stepmother was overjoyed at the brilliant match I was making, as everyone told her, and she was reconciled with me once and for all, although even earlier, since my illness, our relations had been somewhat warmer, and we were gradually working our way toward friendship. I left the baroness's house and several days before my wedding moved into an apartment rented for me in the same building where my stepmother lived. For some incomprehensible reason I couldn't decide whether to tell Bertini about my enmity with Milkot and the terrible scene that had ended my last quarrel with him. My stepmother tearfully begged that I allow Milkot to see me; I didn't object and agreed. He came, calm and cold as usual, offering his hand in silence. I extended my own, suppressing the conflicting emotions roused in me by his presence, and we chatted about the most inconsequential subjects. Remember that my stepmother was poor, as was Milkot, and I, by the will of fate, was already surrounded by luxury and would soon become wealthy. How could I abandon them? I forgave them.

My marriage was approaching. Bertini spared no expense in redoing his house; from morning to night he was kept busy with these matters and other preparations. He hastened the wedding day, burning with impatience. Milkot took it upon himself to help; Bertini accepted the offer willingly, since he wanted to spend more time with me. He treated me in a manner more passionate than tender. Never will I forget the last evening before our wedding: as he was leaving, he suddenly embraced me and, failing to notice my stubborn resistance, kissed me. Oh, that was no tender, meek, unruffled display of affection – like my Michel's caress – but rather an insane kiss, one that seemed to singe me. I quickly freed myself from his arms and, covering my face with my hands, burst into bitter tears. I shared neither his ecstasy nor his rapture – he simply frightened me; his kisses and hugs were painful for me to bear. He was staggered by my tears and confusion, and genuinely reproached himself for his ardor. After he left, I sat sadly in my room for a long time; it was a difficult moment, a time for reflection. I regretted having given my consent and could barely calm myself. The next day I became his wife.

The first days of our marriage remain in my memory like some confused, painful dream. His passion was alien to me; moreover, I had not a single moment of oblivion – an icy coldness remained implacably alive within me. I belonged to him and could do no more than endure his caresses with a painful sense of obligation. If his love had been less demanding, less ardent, perhaps I could have eventually reconciled myself to it. But from the very beginning of my marriage it lay upon me like a weight, under which my whole heart suffered. My natural timidity and my entire organism rebelled inexorably against an assertion of his rights that remained unsanctified by either warm reciprocity or the delicate sensitivity of a truly loving man. His ecstasy and rapture were alien to me – I regarded them coldly; in addition, there were moments when they became hateful. However, I submitted and said not a single word to let my husband know how much I suffered; I myself often attributed this feeling to inexperience at the first shock of my new situation. My husband, devoted exclusively to love, didn't understand and couldn't even guess; his ardent caresses, instead of gradually awakening and arousing feeling in me, merely repelled me. The more effort I made to force myself to endure them patiently, the more painful they became. With each passing day my loathing of married life increased. Concentrated on myself, I had no strength to respond in any way to his endless raptures. True, I was always equally meek and obeyed him in everything, but that was insufficient. He complained that I had no desires; of course, he would have submitted lovingly to all my whims, but I had none to offer. In addition, our house was so lavish, everything so well appointed, it would have been difficult for me to desire anything more. All that luxury was unnecessary; I made use of it with indifference, never quite getting accustomed to it or feeling any particular affection for it. It didn't strike me as either enviable or attractive. My stepmother and Milkot, who was given a post in my husband's office, lived in the same house with us; I rarely saw Milkot, but my stepmother, who loved the pleasures of society, willingly shared them with me or, more accurately, took advantage of them herself. There was a succession of dinners, balls, and parties. I made an impression wherever we went, and praise for my beauty flattered my husband's vanity. Triumphant, he was always at my side. Often, as he sat beside me on our way home, he would say:

"Nina, you look lovely! So lovely! Everyone envied me, Nina! And you're mine – do you understand how much bliss there is in that word?"

"My friend," I said quietly and with effort, "I know you love me."

"I do! I love you madly!"

And he would take my head in his hands and kiss me avidly. I was always embarrassed – and sometimes became despondent for no reason at all. Whenever he noticed, he had different reactions: either he doubled his caresses or suddenly left me and retired to his own room. Once he said:

"Nina, are you really never going to learn to love me? You're like marble, Nina! You're a terrible woman! Still, I love you enough for two people – both you and me – for everyone!"

Judge for yourselves what I could reply to such words. I wanted to be grateful, and said that I couldn't overcome my own icy temperament and the fatal composure of my heart, which remained, against my will, both deaf and dumb. Yes, not once, not ever did it begin to throb – except from fear, sometimes from an outrage that was totally involuntary, but no less powerful for that. I wasn't strong enough to suppress it – but I never permitted myself to express my true feelings, either by gesture or tone of voice, much less by the words that more than once came close to escaping my lips against my will. My main concern, and a consolation, was Lenochka. In my husband's absence, I would spend the whole morning with her. At first, she was wild, fearful, and morose, but gradually she grew accustomed to me and became totally attached. From her own account, I learned that she didn't remember her mother and had lived a long time in Florence, where she'd had a lot to bear from her strict aunt and those around her. Later she was brought to Russia and at once placed in a boarding school, where she rarely saw her father and never enjoyed his affection. An abandoned child, she had no concept of family love or a mother's tender care; very early she'd experienced other people's egoism and insensitivity, and endured the cold demands of tutors and the indifference of her peers – the eternal fate of those abandoned among them without a protector. I loved her a great deal and, finding in me a mother's tenderness and affection, she came to love me with all the intensity of her childish heart, all the passion of her southern temperament. She also became the innocent cause of my first disagreements with my husband. When Bertini came home, he almost always found us together. Often he would send his daughter abruptly out of the room and, remaining alone with me, seemed not to notice my dissatisfied or saddened appearance and never commented on it. This treatment of his daughter struck me unfavorably – never a kind word or glance. Once I mentioned to him that I found it painful to see him so devoted to me, but so implacably aloof to his daughter.

"Leave that subject alone," he said, interrupting me. "What is it to you? Let's talk about something else."

"No," I said. "When I became your wife I accepted the obligation to become her mother. It's my duty and my heart's desire. I love her."

"Do you think I don't see that?" he said heatedly. "I see that and know that you love her. You love her more than you do me."

"You should be ashamed of yourself," I said quietly. "How can you compare two such different attachments?"

"There's nothing to compare; there can't be any comparison, that's obvious. You love her and cherish her. If things go on like this, I shall come to hate her – she's stealing my heart from me."

I was silent.

"Why don't you say something?" he asked irascibly. "Answer me."

"What can I say?" I replied sadly. "My life has worked out so strangely: the very thing that in another marriage could lead to greater love and harmony, in mine becomes a source of discord."

"Discord?" he repeated. "Does that mean you're unhappy with me?"

"Did I say that?"

"You didn't, but you thought it – it's all the same. Discord? I'm willing to give my life for a smile from you, a glance, a word. You're the only one who doesn't understand that by now."

"On the contrary, I understand it perfectly well, and I'm very grateful to you."

"I don't need your gratitude – I need your love; I need happiness and mutual affection. You must understand that! . . . That distresses you! My God, you're crying – forgive me. . . . I'm torturing you, madman that I am! What do I want? Nina, forgive me; have pity and don't blame me – I love you so much!"

He began kissing my hands, then he kissed me, and all of a sudden, breaking off these passionate, chaotic caresses, he went to his study. When he returned, he was morose and gloomy.

Such scenes were repeated constantly between us; those rapid changes from love to despair, from affection to restrained anger, were wearing beyond belief. His reproaches, uttered with cold indifference, always concluded with entreaties to forgive him, were just as unrestrained, and I began to desire only one thing – peace and quiet. I was genuinely content only when Lenochka and I were together. Taking care of the child afforded me a respite from all that dissension.

One morning when I was alone, I was informed that Dmitry Z** had arrived and wished to see me. Since his father's business took him to Petersburg all the time, he wasn't often in Moscow and hadn't seen me since my marriage. I received him, and when he began to inquire with friendly concern about my life and well-being, I couldn't bear his gaze and burst into tears. We were sitting side by side, and he was holding my hands, kissing them silently just as my husband entered the room. He turned terribly pale and froze in the doorway. Not at all embarrassed, I introduced him to Dmitry. He treated him in such a cold, aloof manner that shortly afterward Dmitry took his leave. As soon as he'd left the room, I looked at my husband. He was pacing back and forth in silence.

"Albert," I said, approaching him. "What's the matter?"

He remained silent.

"Albert, tell me, answer me, what's in your heart?"

"Leave me," he said suddenly, pushing me away. "What do you want? You ask what I feel? Instead you ought to ask how I managed to restrain myself? Who was that man?"

"Dmitry Z**, I've already told you."

"Does that really tell me anything? What do I know? When you told me about your past, you were careful never to mention the name of the man you loved. Oh, women, women, you're all the same!"

He burst out laughing. I sat in silence, wounded to the quick by his suspicion. He approached me so menacingly that I threw myself back against the sofa.

"You're silent! So it's true," he said in a thunderous voice. "It didn't take you long to decide to renew old ties. You know, I'm not one of those complaisant husbands – I'll kill you." TF

I stood up and tried to leave the room. He seized my arm and threw me down on the sofa.

"Stay here," he said, "and answer me. Who is he?"

"Listen," I said to him, coldly and abruptly. "I shouldn't have to explain, but I feel sorry for you. I pity your insane impulses. That's the only reason I'll tell you. No, he's not the one."

"What's the other man's name?" he asked, his lips quivering and pale.

"I won't tell you."

"Tell me at once."

"Bertini," I said, getting up. "That tone, those words are worthy neither of you nor me. Come to your senses, you're forgetting the respect you owe me as well as your own dignity. You should be ashamed – I don't deserve such treatment."

My words, uttered proudly and firmly, stunned him. He rapidly moved from jealousy to repentance and implored me to forgive him. But in his eyes I could see all the suspicions he was trying to suppress but that still remained against his will. Therefore, I told him the name of Michel B** and was compelled, in speaking of Dmitry Z**, to soften the impact of my words and explain our relationship. Bertini calmed down.

In that way, or almost, we continued our mutual existence. Two years after my marriage I gave birth to a daughter, my sweet Idochka. But once again my health suffered and for a long time after her birth I was unable to recover. My husband, in spite of my opposition, called for a medical consultation. The doctors found that my constitution had been shaken to the core and urged me to go abroad, fearing the onset of a wasting fever. They conferred with my husband a long time, advising him to look after me and take me abroad immediately. I didn't want to go – I felt that physical weakness when one doesn't want any changes; this state often leads people to prefer to die quietly in place rather than to make the effort to save themselves by undertaking some activity or journey. But my husband didn't hesitate for a minute; he entrusted all his business affairs to Milkot, in whom he had great faith, and, making all the necessary arrangements, took me away. As the horses carried us beyond the gates of Moscow on the Petersburg road, I sat hunched in a corner of the carriage, and, after lowering my veil, wept quietly – still saddened by separation from my children. I couldn't take Idochka with me – she was only six months old – and, despite my pleas, my husband wouldn't allow me to take Lena. I was distracted from my profound self-absorption by his sonorous, brusque voice.

"Nina," he said to me, embracing me, failing to notice my grief. "Now you're all mine. I'm so happy, Nina! At last you're with me. I've carried you off – nothing can come between us. You're mine alone."

I realized that he was talking about the children, and those words made a strong impression on me, forcing me to acknowledge at last how much pure egotism there was in his love for me. For the first time I didn't feel guilty for being cold to him; it occurred to me that love of that sort was merely tyranny and torment, and merited neither gratitude nor sympathy. I remained silent; seeing my immobility, he continued:

"Nina, you've felt such tenderness and affection for the children, and had such a flood of words for them as you parted – have you really none left for me? Say something."

"I can't speak," I said. "My heart still aches over the separation from my children. Let me compose myself."

"Yes, yes, do. But for now, only look at me, kiss me."

I quietly turned my head toward him, making an effort to control myself, and kissed him sadly. All of a sudden he pushed me away forcefully.

"Ah!" he said. "She belongs entirely to others. I'm taking her body away, but her heart and soul remain behind. There's only a lifeless frame left here, a corpse! For me she has only duty and submission – hateful submission – and icy caresses on command. Be careful, Nina, I could learn to hate you." MEN

I remained silent. Confined for over an hour to the cramped space of the carriage, and separated by an abyss of conflicting emotions and sensations, we sat gloomily side by side, avoiding each other's glance and most likely cursing the incongruity between our two characters, the gradual development of which increasingly offended him and created in me a sense of alienation. However, in accordance with the progression of feelings that I had come to know so well, later that day he begged my forgiveness with the same passion with which he'd offended me several hours earlier. Exhausted by his incessant emotional outbursts, I made my peace with him, if not tranquilly, then at least as he demanded, immediately, without reproaches or complaints. But every time I felt more strongly the tug of my chain and the painful distress it caused me. I won't go into our travels in great detail; the warmth of the south, the radiant sky, the bright sun, and luxuriant nature revived me. I grew healthier and became more cheerful, while Bertini calmed down and tormented me less. In Italy I discovered a new ability I hadn't known I possessed: faced with expressions of beauty, I forgot all about my grief. In whatever form it appeared, I delighted in beauty beyond all measure. I forgot everything on earth as I wept at the opera, as I strolled beneath the pink rays of the fading evening sun that illuminated Roman monuments and ancient walls with a fantastic play of colors, and as, in astonishment and exaltation, I stood before paintings and statues. I formed habits to which I devoted myself with youthful enthusiasm: at a fixed time I would set off for one of Rome's many palaces. There I would sit opposite a painting that I particularly admired and lose myself in contemplation of it, experiencing a placid, refined pleasure equal to happiness. My husband watched me jealously, but rejoiced in my reawakening to life and greedily seized on those moments of animation for his own ends. Our life flowed along more tranquilly and evenly; but evidently I was to be granted no rest, because a new incident destroyed everything and subjected us once again to all the agitation of the barely becalmed storm.

It was a splendid evening in April. I was sitting by the window, looking off into the distance at the green hill of the Pincio. We were living on the Piazza di Spagna. I suddenly had an irresistible urge to go for a walk. I stood up and put on my hat.

"Where are you going, Nina?" my husband asked.

"Out for a stroll," I replied.

"You just refused me when I invited you to go to the Corso," he said.

"I don't like noisy streets. There are very few people on the Pincio now. I'll be back soon," I said.

"I'll go with you."

"Why, my dear? You wanted to go the Café Greco. I'll be back in half an hour."

"No, I'll go with you," he said again.

I wanted to be alone, but I yielded to his wish and we went together. We made our way slowly up the hill hand in hand. I was in a tranquil frame of mind and said little, fully enjoying myself and avidly breathing in the cool evening air. A man came walking toward us; when he was only a few paces away I began trembling and choked back an involuntary exclamation.

"What's wrong, Nina? What's the matter with you?" my husband asked.

"Nothing," I said, regaining control.

But my hand shook terribly; he squeezed it and, glancing up, saw the seemingly frozen figure of the man standing in front of us, staring at me in consternation. We walked on, leaving him still standing there. I couldn't go any farther and sat down on the nearest bench; the trembling, horror, and agitation took my breath away – the shock was severe, all the more so because it was so unexpected.

"That's Michel B",," said my husband, mercilessly looking me right in the eye. "I recognized him from the hatred that welled up in me and the agitation that overcame you. Answer me."

"I want to go home," I said in a faint voice.

He led me back down the hill in silence, and we returned home. Then his terrible, insane jealousy exploded over me. He accused me caustically of seeking that meeting; he said that was why I wanted to go out alone and tried to dissuade him from accompanying me; I had probably known for some time that he was in Rome and had been seeing him in secret. For the first time I lost my habitual coldness; I rebelled against his cruelty and said:

"Does your love really resemble any true feeling? It's my eternal torment. I can't understand love without trust, love by force. Leave me alone – your love is no more than pure egotism. You don't know what love means!"

He was stunned by the words that burst forth so angrily after my passing confusion. He rushed out of the room like a madman and didn't return home that night. I feared both for him and for Michel, and passed a most horrible night. I knew that in a fit of jealousy he was capable of anything. In the morning he returned. I went into his study intending to ask that we leave Rome immediately. When he saw me, he didn't give me a chance to utter a single word. He said abruptly, without even looking at me:

"Pack your things. We're leaving this evening."

I tried to speak . . .

"Not a word. We're leaving this evening!" *HO*

I was offended by the way he addressed me. I had come to see him to request precisely what he had ordered so tyrannically, and that in itself outraged me.

We left Rome mutually aware that we could no longer lead such an existence. I had found in him nothing that could reconcile me with him afterward. I knew already that he possessed not even one of the qualities that would enable me to find points of contact and sympathy in our life together, but now I could no longer forgive him for his crude love for me, and, even less, for his fantastic jealousy. Our life had become a source of anguish, interrupted only by contemptible scenes that neither faded quickly nor were short-lived, as they had been in the first year of our marriage. Often my pensiveness or exhaustion became a new pretext for storm; he asked me in a threatening manner, with the intolerance of an Italian and the unbridled nature of a jealous man: "What are you thinking about?" I would reply either with scornful coldness or totally uncharacteristic passion. My whole being rebelled against such moral violence and protested loudly against his intolerance that encroached upon my inner world. Then he would leave me, hurling reproaches and sarcastic remarks, wounding the secret, sacred depths of my heart.

At the time we were living in Baden.* He began to play roulette frequently at the spa. At first I didn't quite grasp this new misfortune and regarded it from a different point of view, taking it as a relief because he often left me alone. Our relations changed – there were fewer quarrels, but more coldness and alienation. There were also moments of reconciliation and emotional outpourings on his part, but I knew they wouldn't last and were not altogether genuine. I recognized that his passion was fading with each passing day; sometimes there remained only the desire to possess a woman whose beauty he still cherished, and that alone brought him to my feet. This new insult eradicated any trace of amicable gratitude I felt. I submitted to him, but already with decreasing respect for his moral aspect, and I was often surprised by the small alteration of mood that could make him forget so quickly all our past troubles, assuming that I felt the same way.

After we had spent two years abroad, we returned to Russia. The meeting with my children was illuminated with the joy that floods the heart of a woman who recognizes that they alone are alive for her and represent her hope for the future, a basis for reconciliation, and her sole consolation. I was much better, but not entirely recovered. I was certain that the constant fear of the new quarrels that arose frequently, as well as my own agitation at each new squabble, had a great impact on my organism and significantly reduced the benefit I gained from my travels. After we returned to Russia, my husband had even less mercy on me, and I myself moved from extreme exhaustion to sudden changes of mood: I became willful and morbidly irritable; I felt less sorry for him and judged him more harshly. He was gloomy at home, and in the evenings always went to his club and dedicated himself to gambling with the same passion he brought to all his whims and tastes. I no longer had much influence over him – it was diminishing, passing noticeably into Milkot's hands; he had managed the household and business affairs in our absence, and retained control of them after our return as well. At first, not for my own benefit but for our daughters, I struggled against Milkot's growing power and tried to keep Bertini at home, divert him from gambling, and distance him from Milkot. But my efforts yielded little and only stopped my husband for a short time. Finally my requests ceased having any influence over him. When I talked to him about Milkot, he didn't want to hear it and stubbornly insisted that the only reason I didn't like Milkot was that he was so genuinely attached to him. Often a bitter gibe would end our argument, and, after a harsh reproach, he would leave me. All this sapped my energy, and it decreased. Two more years spent in family squabbles and misgivings, even about our financial future, and the impossibility of deflecting my husband from the slippery path he had embarked upon, led me to acknowledge my powerlessness in the long run. I bowed to my fate, bore my painful life with a slavish silence, the hopelessness of a prisoner locked away for life, the submissiveness of a child; each day I waited for some new misfortune. It was not long in coming. One morning Milkot came in to see me.

"Antonina Mikhailovna," he said, "would you be so kind as to inform your husband that he's on the verge of ruin? Yesterday he gambled away an enormous sum of money. Soon it will be the first of the month – payments are coming due and there's not much money left in the office. If this goes on much longer, we'll be bankrupt."

"My God!" I said, standing up. "Have we really reached that point?"

"Indeed we have," replied Milkot. "What have you been thinking about? Since he came back, I've been left to mind his affairs while he gambles. That's not the worst of it: the point is, he's taking dreadful losses."

"You're master over him," I said. "Why don't you stop him? Why turn to me? You know that you're partly to blame for the change in his attitude toward me."

"Not in the least," he replied. "You alone are to blame for everything. My influence over him begins and ends in business matters, but your indifference to your marital obligations has driven him to an insane passion for gambling. We owe this general misfortune to you."

"Keep still," I said. "That doesn't concern you. If we're ruined, only the children and I will suffer for it. You're obligated to my husband for five years of independence; you've lived here in luxury. The estate belongs to him alone; consequently, he has the right to squander it, if he so chooses."

"That's so, but not entirely. It's true that I've held an advantageous position in his office; but the point is that during the first years of your marriage, my wife and I turned our capital over to Bertini. If he's bankrupt, then we'll lose the fruits of our whole life's labors."

"Then take your capital back now," I said.

"You don't understand what commercial turnover means; when business is bad, it's impossible to take money out – there isn't any. If he stops gambling, he may still be able to recover. He already owes a number of people; I haven't taken the interest owed me for the last two years, and now . . . "

"Now what?" I repeated in horror, seeing the abyss before my eyes.

"The percentage has grown, of course. I don't know how he'll pay us. When I told him about it, he asked me to wait; but if I insist on it now and present my promissory note for payment, it would sound a general alarm and ruin him. If I present it, all his debtors will descend on him at once."

"Have you asked for your money back?"

"Many times. He says he can't settle with me right now."

"All right," I said. "I'll speak to him."

Bertini came home for dinner, his face pale and gloomy. When he came into the room, I was sitting with the children. I sent them away at once.

"Albert," I said, going up to him. "I would like to speak with you."

"What do you want?" he asked, not looking at me.

I stopped, collecting my thoughts and summoning up all my resolution. The formal way he spoke was not promising and showed me how irritated he was.

"If you prefer, I'll talk to you later, another day, when you're feeling calmer."

"I'm calm. Today or tomorrow, it makes no difference. Say what you have to say."

"Today I was informed that your business affairs are going badly," I uttered timidly.

"That may be," he replied quietly.

"Listen," I said. "You know that I don't need a thing. I lived in poverty before and I can do so again, but you must consider your daughters and your good name – you'll be bankrupt, that's horrible. There's no money left, yet you still gamble and lose. How many times have I asked you to moderate this passion? All my entreaties have been in vain."

"I'm not bankrupt yet. I still have enough to settle honestly with everyone."

"What about your daughters?" I objected. "Does this mean there'll be nothing left for them?"

"My daughters," he said with sudden heat. "Do I have any daughters? I'm almost sure that the first one isn't mine – I raised her out of pity; and the second, most likely, isn't mine either. You were so preoccupied with that other man when you were pregnant that she was born blond and pale, just like the man you loved. I saw him, I know – what kind of daughter is she to me?"

"Albert!" I said imploringly.

"What? Isn't it the truth? Who's to blame for all our misfortunes, if not you? Yes, you, you alone! I failed to arouse in you heart, mind, or feeling! You were like a statue in my arms; not once, not a single time did your icy shell melt from my love. Tell me, have you ever really been my wife? Perhaps you only imagined it? Can a woman taken in marriage who merely tolerates and endures her husband ever really be his wife? Can a woman who belongs yet doesn't give herself, who secretly but endlessly objects to her husband's rights – can she be called his wife?"

"When have I ever complained?" I objected.

"But your silence, your coldness, your melancholy – weren't they an eloquent, endless protest? While you were in my embrace, weren't you always dreaming of someone else – as if you were futilely saving your life, love, rapture, and bliss for him, damn him! Weren't you heartless and unresponsive with me? Is such a woman really a wife? What do you think?"

"Albert," I said, "didn't I tell you I could only love you as a friend? Why do you accuse me of a crime for the very thing I warned you about? Remember how long I refused to marry you?"

"That's true. But then you seemed different in my eyes: you stood unattainably high. Later I learned a great deal about you; moreover, when you told me about your great romance, didn't you assure me that you were no longer in love with your former lover?"

"My lover?" I said indignantly. "What right do you have to say that to me?"

"Yes, your lover – how else can I refer to the man who took complete possession not only of your heart, but of all your emotions? You continued to see him always and, who knows . . . "

"Bertini – not one more word," I said. "I'm ashamed of you."

He jumped up from his chair.

"Silence," he cried. "I've put up with a great deal from you – my patience is finally exhausted. Your ingratitude to my constant self-sacrifice . . . "

"Self-sacrifice?" I said. "When exactly?"

"When? When I took you away from Russia, the doctors told me I must care for you and minister to you. Wasn't I thinking only of you then? Loving you madly, I sacrificed myself to you – remember that!"

"I was dying," I said.

"Yes, from love for another, from barren regrets for the past that my own love wasn't powerful enough to destroy. And later, when you recovered your health and resumed your life, what did I find in you? The same unfeeling woman! You complain that I've become a gambler – why did I? Because, while I worshipped you, I loved alone, I loved a statue; I had not one moment of passion, not one moment of oblivion with you. You were as unfeeling as stone, and more than once I cursed both you and myself. My words, assurances, caresses had but one result: they doubled your coldness. A daughter of the north with icy blood in her veins, you were unable to give me that which is said to constitute the charm and fascination of such women: their heart. Tell me, did your heart ever belong to me? Tell me how you repaid my love for you."

"I gave your children a mother. I repaid you with sincere friendship – anything else wasn't within my power to give," I replied.

"I have no children, I tell you, and I've always disdained and hated your friendship. Now I'll tell you the whole truth – it's been oppressing me and stinging me for a long time. I hate you as the perpetrator of all my misfortunes and curse the hour when I was so insane as to join my fate with yours – not with a woman, but with an automaton that moves without aim, will, or desire in my home."

I sat down in a chair, crushed by the weight of his words.

"And how do I know," he continued in a burst of rage and indignation, "how do I know that you hadn't kept up your previous relations? Did you see him after we returned to Russia?"

I remained silent.

"Did you see him or not?"

"I didn't seek an opportunity to see him," I replied.

"So, they didn't deceive me – you confess it."

"I'm not confessing anything. The truth is merely that I met him in church on two Sundays and saw him once in the park where I was strolling with the children. I stopped going to that park and didn't attend church, and since then I haven't seen him."

"Be careful," he said to me, gasping for breath from agitation. "I no longer love you, but, of course, I won't allow you to besmirch my name. I will break your neck if I discover anything."

Omfg

"I'm not afraid of your threats," I said coldly. "And it doesn't take threats to make me behave properly. I respect myself enough that I won't permit myself to stray from my obligations."

"If you had understood them better," he said to me as he left the room, "we wouldn't have reached this painful point in our life and would never have known the misfortunes that will soon rain down on us."

I was left in total despair. Since that time my life has been a series of uninterrupted torments: both external and internal, in the family and in society. After this conversation my husband continued to gamble and couldn't stop, even though he knew he was standing on the brink of an abyss. Like all gamblers, he was overcome by the hope of recouping his losses; when Milkot confronted him with the disastrous state of his affairs, his answer was always the same: spring will come; so far I've been unlucky, but I'll win it all back, without fail I will, and things will improve.

In the meantime, we owed money to everyone. True, luxury was still apparent in our house, and Bertini supported and displayed it, as if for show, to counter the rumors of financial ruin that had begun to circulate in town. He made me attend balls and redeemed my diamonds, sometimes just for one evening – after which they were pawned again. In the meantime, everything we needed for the house was obtained on credit, and we were often treated to offensive, though justified, remarks from those who came to collect their money and went away deceived in their hopes. Lena and Idochka had no teachers left – I tutored them myself. I was even forced to dismiss their nanny and was left with only one maid, and I owed her a whole year's salary. But why should I enumerate all the petty details, deprivations, and worries amid a luxuriously appointed house – details that poisoned every morsel of bread, and worries that never allowed me to close my eyes in peace at night and that awoke together with me to go on haunting me constantly. Add to this the complete rupture with my husband, the continual reproaches and complaints of my stepmother, who feared losing her capital, Milkot's crude outbursts – and you will have some sense of the hellish life I led at the time. My husband forced me to sign a promissory note for Milkot, which had ballooned, since the interest wasn't paid, to the enormous sum of 15,000 silver rubles (I'm speaking only of my own obligation); he assured Milkot that my diamonds would cover this debt. However, all this proved superfluous. One morning Bertini confiscated the pawn tickets and I don't know what became of those diamonds – whether he gambled them away or used them to pay some other debt.

At long last everything collapsed. Our creditors got tired of waiting. One of them presented a note for payment and it was as if a signal had been given to all the others – a multitude of notes was presented, and my husband was bankrupt. I left the house with nothing of my own, and my husband went abroad, promising to start all over again. He left me to live with my stepmother and Milkot, and when he left repeated my stepmother's words of bygone years: "I entrust you to your family. Since I know that you can't live alone, that you can't control yourself and will do thousands of foolish things, I don't want my name to become an object of gossip and mockery by the crowd. Milkot will look after you."

I strongly and staunchly objected to that verdict, which condemned me to new torments; but I was compelled to submit because I had to choose between this decision and separation from my children. My husband was unyielding – and his answer was always the same: "If you don't want to live with your stepmother and Milkot, I'll take the children."

What could I do – necessity chained me to them; after all the vicissitudes of my life, it was as if I had described a fantastic circle, returning to the point from which I had escaped with such effort after Michel's marriage. Here I see the same play of chance which, governing my entire life, brought me so implacably and against my will to replicate the experience of my youth. I could have found a way out – once you've lost the desire to live, dying offers no difficulties – and, after calm and firm reflection, I could have done it, but once again I was bound by duty. What would become of my daughters? They need me, they love me – this thought concentrated all my remaining energy into moving along the path of life with no excessive expenditure of sensitivity that could weaken my will to live and destroy me. Milkot presented his promissory note together with the other creditors and received only half the money owed him – now I owe him the rest and am paying the interest by giving lessons. I'm also repaying bit by bit some of the capital, when I have money left at the end of the year. He continues to despise me, more out of habit, it seems, than feeling, and my stepmother hasn't forgiven me for my husband's ruin, considering me the main cause of our unhappy marriage. She's right, of course – like all those who think it's possible to remake one's character and to live among apathetic and unsympathetic people. Throughout all this one thing has been forgotten – namely, it's impossible to develop independence, just as it's impossible to destroy it; the makeup of our character doesn't depend on us, but is no more than our innate inclinations combined with the way our life develops; it's impossible to love or hate according to any assigned standard. These feelings are as unfettered as clouds, as free as birds – who knows where they come from or where they fly to?

Be that as it may, living in the presence of my stepmother and Milkot, and depending on them for so much, I now have no calm whatever. I live among endless upheavals and alarms, I am subjected to frequent insults, and I don't know when I'll be delivered from all this. During the last years of my marriage, Milkot's only job was supervising my husband's office. He had lost the habit of working, and, finding it possible to live on the interest payments without depriving himself in any way, he didn't want to give lessons now. His idle life has given rise to numerous conflicts between him and my stepmother. She is older than he, and he's long since stopped loving her. Most likely he's developed new ties and attractions; she is jealous and often quarrels with him. Their life is a constant repetition of one and the same argument – she often moves from jealousy to attempts to please him and back again, while he regards it all indifferently. If he's dissatisfied, his bad mood is shifted onto the whole family, and he takes out his marital problems on us. Of course, the children and I suffer more than my stepmother. All my hope now rests on attaining the single blessing still accessible to me – independence, and, consequently, tranquillity. When and how? I don't know – I have no cause for hope; but I'm waiting, most likely, by virtue of that strange capacity, hidden deep inside, that makes a person go on hoping, against all common sense. I value tranquillity highly and think that, after all my misfortunes, I would take a greedy pleasure in it, like people who ruined their youth and all its seductive atmosphere in fruitless upheavals – after which only destruction remains – the dust and ashes of hope! Tranquillity is a great blessing, the only real blessing of a life that's already ended; the carefree sleep of an infant and the immobile figure of an old man warming himself in the sun are, in my opinion, identical: peace comes both before and after the struggle. Extremes converge!

Now, my friends, you know the story of my life. I was in a hurry to end it and told you quickly, in only a few words, the most recent circumstances, the last period of my married life, because I found it so painful to speak of these recent storms. I don't like to delve into this chaos and prefer to leave such storms in the dark regions of my heart. My memory approaches them cautiously, and there is a secret revulsion when my inner world summons them from the obscurity to which my reason has condemned them. It seems to me that my life, taken as a whole, has demanded more strength than I possessed, but I continue to live it in the name of duty – and perhaps also from force of habit, purely mechanically – sometimes with a stoicism rooted in absolute indifference to everything. But, in conclusion I would say: don't judge unhappiness merely by the fact of its existence; everything on earth is measured in relative terms; that which crushed me and made me come out of the ordeal with exhausted soul and strength might at first only cast a tinge of sadness on another, less proud person; she might even be reconciled to much of it and, in so doing, might alter her fate. I was unable to do so; I struggled for a long time – from childhood to the present, and the struggle destroyed me. I confess: I fell – others defeated me. Yet even now my pride is not silent – it stands tall and constantly repeats, like Francis I: all is lost save honor.* Honor of struggle, truth of life, purity of aspiration – these are the things I am left with, and I shall carry this wealth to the grave.

1 *Mainz* – A great historical city in Germany on the left bank of the Rhine opposite the mouth of the Main.

1 *Ninochka* – An affectionate diminutive form of the name Antonina.

2 *Milkot* – This name is borrowed from Millcote, a town in Charlotte Brontë's novel *Jane Eyre* (1847), and shows Tur's high regard for Brontë's work.

22 *verst* – A Russian unit of measurement equal to 3,500 feet.

27 *Ilmenev and Pletneev* – Characters from Tur's novel (see translator's note) to whom she relates her life story in the episode *Antonina*. Here these figures function primarily as hearers of the tale.

31 *barège* – A gauzy fabric woven from worsted and silk or cotton; used for veils, etc.

33 *sylph* – A slender or graceful woman; from a system devised by the Swiss physician and alchemist Paracelsus (1493?–1541), referring to a class of mortal, but soulless, beings supposed to inhabit the air.

33 *governess* – Typically from the impoverished nobility; thus, while not strictly from a different class, they were generally considered to be of lower social status.

34 *troika* – A Russian carriage drawn by three horses abreast.

38 *Shrovetide* – Three days before Ash Wednesday set aside as a special season of festivity before the beginning of Lent.

41 *stove-bench* – A shelf running alongside a Russian stove on which it is possible to sleep.

43 *samovar* – A metal urn used to boil water for tea.

44 *Schiller* – A quotation from Friedrich Schiller's play *The Robbers* (*Die Raüber*) (1781), act 1, scene 2.

47 *fretted pictures* – Borders with an ornamental pattern of small, straight lines intersecting or joining one another at right angles to form a regular design.

72 *quadrille* – A dance of French origin in which four or eight couples dance in a square; it became extremely popular in nineteenth-century European society.

80 *civil servant* – In 1722 Peter the Great reorganized the administration of Russia and introduced a table of ranks for the civil service. Consent of a superior was required before a civil servant could marry.

92 *Laocoön's children* – In Greek legend Laocoön was a priest of Apollo who warned the Trojans not to accept the wooden horse left by the Greeks during the Trojan War. Two sea serpents sent by the gods killed Laocoon and his two sons.

102 *Mamenka* – Michel refers to his aunt by a Russian diminutive for "Mother," thus showing the closeness of their relationship. Antonina also once refers to the aunt as Michel's mother.

112 *faro* – A gambling game in which players bet on the cards to be turned up from the top of the dealer's pack.

114 *French colony* – A section of town where foreigners tended to live.

115 *Ostozhenka* – A street in Moscow.

132 *Pincio, Piazza di Spagna, Corso* – Locations in Rome.

134 *Baden* – A picturesque town in Switzerland noted for its sulfur baths.

145 *honor* – Francis I (1494–1547), King of France, wrote these words to his mother after losing the Battle of Pavia (1525) to Charles V in the Italian Wars. It is said that Napoleon repeated them after his military defeat at the Battle of Waterloo (1815).

Excerpt from a Review by Ivan Turgenev

There seems to be no reason to assure our readers of the deep sympathy aroused in us by the talent of Madame Tur. On the other hand, they can also see that this sympathy is not blind, and that, without a moment's hesitation, we have expressed our opinion about what has seemed to be the less successful aspect of her work; therefore, we hope that our readers will not be suspicious of the warm praise with which we welcome the story of Antonina, particularly its first half. These pages – we say with firm conviction – will remain in Russian literature. They – perhaps! – will enter the ranks of those select poetic inventions which have become our own, domestic ones, which we love to ponder, a liking for which eventually becomes a habit closely connected with the very best of our recollections. The content of such fortunate inventions is almost always uncomplicated: it is simple, like the very fundamentals of life. We called these inventions fortunate: their good fortune consists not in the novelty of the unheard-of nature of the main idea, but in the fact that life has been given to it, that it has opened its sources and willingly flowed along with its bright wave. All the originality and uncommonness consist in this. Life does not respond to every summons: Aladdin's magic lamp, before which everything is gladly revealed, is delivered into the hands of very few, even among poets. We'll say more: it often falls to people who don't possess that much talent. We recall the Abbé Prévost and his *Manon Lescaut*,[1] Bernardin de Saint-Pierre and his *Paul et Virginie*.[2] It is rather difficult to define the conditions of such good fortune: they are connected with the lives of the fortunate ones. But we must state that a certain, rather powerful reflection of this good fortune – the good fortune to create a simple image, one not condemned to fade – fell to the lot of the author of *Antonina*. We would like to believe that Antonina will not be forgotten – the first years of her youth, her love for Michel with all the enchanting freshness and charm of first attachments, the bashful triumph of unanticipated bliss, and the heart-rending grief of her sudden separation. All this is written simply, with feeling, in an offhand manner, as Madame Tur usually writes, and as, by the way, we observe incidentally, *Manon Lescaut* is written. But the same offhandedness of form in the story of Antonina is a delight. The aspiring, sincere passion seeks no expressions and finds none: they rush to meet her.

We cared less for the ending of the story, beginning with the appearance of Mr. Bertini, an Italian with a powerful temperament and melodramatic proclivities. Antonina's relationship to him is not quite natural and a bit strained, and somehow unpleasantly destroys the harmony of the impression created in the reader by the first half of the tale.

The review was written in 1852. This excerpt was translated by Michael R. Katz from I. S. Turgenev, *Polnoe sobranie sochinenii* (Moscow and Leningrad: Academy of Sciences, 1963), vol. 5, pp. 382–83.

1. Antoine François Prévost d'Exiles, known as Abbé Prévost (1697–1763), was a French novelist, journalist, and cleric. His most popular work was one of a series of seven novels: *Manon Lescaut*

(1728–32) is an account of the passion of a likable but weak young man for a woman whose frivolity leads him to crime.

2. Jacques Henri Bernardin de Saint-Pierre (1737–1814) was a French naturalist, writer, and friend of Rousseau. His most popular novel, *Paul et Virginie* (1787), is a romantic idyll of two young lovers in a tropical Eden.

»»» SELECTED BIBLIOGRAPHY «««

Costlow, Jane T. "Speaking the Sorrow of Women: Turgenev's 'Neschastnaia' and Evgeniia Tur's 'Antonina.'" *Slavic Review* 50, no. 2 (Summer 1991): 328–35.

Gheith, Jehanne. "In Her Own Voice: Evgeniia Tur, Author, Critic, Journalist." Ph.D. diss., Stanford University, 1992.

———. "Redefining the Perceptible: The Journalism(s) of Evgeniia Tur and Avdot'ia Panaeva." In *Women and Journalism in Imperial Russia*. Ed. J. Gheith and B. Norton. Durham, N.C.: Duke University Press, forthcoming.

———. "The Superfluous Man and the Necessary Woman: 'A Re-vision.'" *Russian Review* 55 (April 1996): 226–44.

———. "Tur, Evgéniia." In *Dictionary of Russian Women Writers*. Ed. M. Ledkovsky, C. Rosenthal, and M. Zirin. Westport, Conn.: Greenwood Press, 1994. 667–72.

Heldt, Barbara. "The Russian Heroine: Where to Find Her and Where Not To." In *Terrible Perfection: Women and Russian Literature*. Bloomington: Indiana University Press, 1987. 12–24.

European Classics

Honoré de Balzac
The Bureaucrats

Heinrich Böll
Absent without Leave
And Never Said a Word
And Where Were You, Adam?
The Bread of Those Early Years
End of a Mission
Irish Journal
Missing Persons and Other Essays
The Safety Net
A Soldier's Legacy
The Stories of Heinrich Böll
The Train Was on Time
What's to Become of the Boy?
Women in a River Landscape

Madeleine Bourdouxhe
La Femme de Gilles

Karel Čapek
Nine Fairy Tales
War with the Newts

Lydia Chukovskaya
Sofia Petrovna

Grazia Deledda
After the Divorce
Elias Portolu

Yury Dombrovsky
The Keeper of Antiquities

Aleksandr Druzhinin
Polinka Saks • The Story
of Aleksei Dmitrich

Venedikt Erofeev
Moscow to the End of the Line

Konstantin Fedin
Cities and Years

Fyodor Vasilievich Gladkov
Cement

I. Grekova
The Ship of Widows

Marek Hlasko
The Eighth Day of the Week

Bohumil Hrabal
Closely Watched Trains

Erich Kästner
Fabian: The Story of a Moralist

Valentine Kataev
Time, Forward!

Ignacy Krasicki
The Adventures of Mr. Nicholas Wisdom

Miroslav Krleza
The Return of Philip Latinowicz

Curzio Malaparte
Kaputt

Karin Michaëlis
The Dangerous Age

Andrey Platonov
The Foundation Pit

Bolesław Prus
The Sins of Childhood and Other Stories